THE GREATEST STORY
UNTOLD
WINTER IN PARIS

BOOK 2 VOLUME 1

PARIS D.

Print ISBN: 978-1-63616-245-4
eBook ISBN: 978-1-63616-246-1

Published By Opportune Independent Publishing Co.

Printed in the United States of America

For permission requests, please email the publisher with the subject line as "Attention: Permissions Coordinator" to the email address below:
Info@Opportunepublishing.com

Mood: Grateful
Song: Muni Long
Superpowers

Table of Contents

ANAM CARA

Anam is the Gaolic word for soul; *cara* is the word for friend.
So anam cara means soul friend.

"The anam cara was a person to whom you could reveal hidden intimacies of your life. This friendship was an act of recognition and belonging."

— John O'Donohue

A Message From the Universe

"For years, the ancient ones have watched over the world with solemn eyes, waiting for the right moment to restore order.

Their wisdom and power were beyond measure, yet they remained hidden, biding their time until the balance of the world was threatened once more. They understood that the corrupt forces of the flesh and the pure essence of the spirit were headed towards a collision course with catastrophic consequences. It was now up to a chosen few to heed the call and unravel the secrets of the ancient ones, for their knowledge holds the key to saving Mother Earth from impending doom."

Chapter 1

SAVE MOTHER EARTH!

The Flesh vs. the Spirit

The Safe House: Somewhere in Georgia

In a dimly lit basement, a group of unlikely allies huddled around a flickering lantern. Their faces were shadowed with uncertainty, yet an unspoken understanding bound them together in this impromptu refuge. Miami, the youngest of them, who was barely twenty-two, broke the silence.

"Where is Paris? And has Samantha had any water or food?" Miami asked. She tapped her foot impatiently, scanning the dimly lit room with a piercing gaze. Across the room, Tokyo sat hunched over, scribbling furiously in her worn notebook.

"I don't know where Paris is," Tokyo replied curtly, flipping a page without looking up. "And Fatima and Kay Slay—they haven't come back, either." She waved a hand dismissively, ignoring the question about Samantha's well-being.

Miami's patience snapped. "We can't keep waiting around!" she hissed, the tension evident in her tone. "I have other things to handle. I'm nobody's babysitter, but it feels like I'm babysitting you—and her!" With that, Miami spun on her heel and stormed out, slamming the door behind her. The sound echoed through the narrow hallway, leaving Tokyo alone in the oppressive silence.

Tokyo smirked while she placed her notebook aside. "Now, the real fun begins," she muttered, reaching under the bed to retrieve a battered and charred blowtorch. The metal was warm in her hand, memories flickering as she stared at it.

Her eyes glinted with a sinister light while she knelt and pried open a loose floorboard, revealing a metal box hidden beneath. She ran her fingers over the box's worn surface, feeling the dents and scratches—each one a piece of its mysterious history.

Across the room, Samantha's eyes widened in terror. Duct tape sealed her mouth shut, muffling her panicked cries. Her wrists and ankles were bound tightly to a chair. She thrashed against the restraints, but it was futile.

"No! Please, no!" Samantha tried to scream, her voice muffled while tears streamed down her cheeks. She watched in horror while Tokyo ignited the blowtorch, the blue-orange flames casting flickering shadows across the room.

Tokyo chuckled darkly. "Time to unveil my masterpiece," she murmured, inching closer to Samantha with the blowtorch roaring in her hand. Samantha's heart pounded violently, while the acrid smell of burning metal filled the air.

Meanwhile, in Miami's SUV

Miami gripped the steering wheel tightly, frustration bubbling beneath her calm exterior. "How the hell did I lose Diego's trail?" she muttered, glancing at her Apple CarPlay screen. She hit redial, but the call went straight to voicemail. "Zeke, pick up!" she growled before abruptly hanging up.

Miami sighed, her thoughts racing. "I may have to call Yasmeen," she said reluctantly, knowing it was a last resort. Yasmeen was resourceful but always came with complications.

While she dialed the private number, she braced herself. On the third ring, Yasmeen's sultry voice answered. "Yasmeen speaking. I knew you'd come back to Mama. Miss me, love?" Yasmeen teased, her voice laced with amusement.

"Cut the crap, Yasmeen," Miami snapped. "I need your help. This is serious."

Yasmeen paused, the playful tone fading. "All right. Come meet me in Moscow. Wear something sexy—I've missed those lips," she said with a chuckle that grated on Miami's nerves.

"Yasmeen, focus!" Miami barked, with exasperation.

Yasmeen sighed, her voice turning serious. "Fine. I'll send you the location. Keep a low profile. We can't afford any more attention."

Moments later, Miami's phone buzzed with a text:
Location: Private Airstrip

Miami rolled her eyes but felt a flicker of relief. "Too easy," she muttered, still wary. "I better be ready for war when I see her," she muttered, her wariness growing while she turned onto Lucky Street, her SUV purring beneath her.

Fifteen minutes later

Miami stepped onto the tarmac, her presence commanding attention like the heroine of an epic saga. She wore a stunning Versace masterpiece—an exclusive runway edition coat crafted with precision and opulence. The coat was a blend of white and soft beige mink fur, its texture a luxurious harmony of warmth and elegance. Intricate leather panels, embossed with Versace's iconic Greek key design, ran along the seams, adding a contemporary edge. The coat's dramatic silhouette flowed gracefully around her, the hem brushing her knees as the gold-plated buttons gleamed in the moonlight.

The collar was a statement on its own—a wide, plush mink shawl that framed her neck and highlighted her sharp cheekbones. Around her waist, a fitted leather belt cinched her frame, adorned with a striking Medusa-head buckle, a subtle nod to the house of Versace. While Miami moved, the coat caught the light, shimmering softly, a testament to its handcrafted precision and exclusivity.

Her matching Versace fur boots, lined with the same soft mink as her coat, completed the ensemble. The boots were adorned with delicate golden zippers that traced up the sides, each pull tab engraved with the iconic Versace emblem. Miami's appearance wasn't just chic—it was an unapologetic statement of power.

Boarding Yasmeen's $500 Million-Dollar G650ER

When Miami ascended the staircase to Yasmeen's private jet, it was clear this was no ordinary aircraft. This customized G650ER was the epitome of airborne luxury, a flying palace designed for royalty and moguls. The exterior, a sleek matte black with Yasmeen's insignia in gold, glistened under the runway lights. Every detail whispered extravagance.

Inside, the jet was a world of its own. The entryway was adorned with custom Italian marble floors, a breathtaking contrast to the ambient soft lighting that mimicked the glow of a sunset. Miami's heels clicked softly as she stepped into the main cabin, her eyes sweeping over the opulent space.

The walls were paneled with polished ebony wood inlaid with gold accents, while the ceiling featured a fiber-optic display that mirrored the constellations of the night sky. The seating area boasted oversized Hermès leather recliners, their cream tones exuding warmth and elegance. Each seat had its own touchscreen control panel for climate, lighting, and a library of on-demand entertainment.

The jet's lounge area featured a plush sectional sofa upholstered in cashmere and silk blends, paired with a low-slung table crafted from crystal and gold. A fully stocked bar lined one side, illuminated by recessed lighting. Rows of Lalique crystal decanters housed rare spirits, while the accompanying glasses sparkled like gemstones.

While Miami made her way to the private master suite, she marveled at its understated grandeur. The king-sized bed was dressed in Fretted linens, and the headboard, upholstered in soft white leather, bore Yasmeen's initials embroidered in gold. The suite also included an en suite bathroom with a rainfall shower, gold-plated fixtures, and a vanity stocked with the most exclusive skincare products.

Miami finally reached her cabin, designed to be a retreat within this airborne kingdom. It was insulated for absolute silence, with dark, soothing tones and blackout curtains ensuring privacy and comfort. A tray of fresh ginger ale and exotic fruit awaited her on a side table, accompanied by a handwritten note from Yasmeen:
> ***For my favorite complication. See you soon, love.***
>
> *— Y*

Settling into her seat, Miami let herself sink into the plush embrace of the chair. The engines purred to life, their low hum vibrating through the floor, as the jet began to taxi down the runway. Outside, the city lights blurred into streaks of gold, and the stars seemed to bow as the jet soared skyward.

With the altitude climbing and the hum of luxury surrounding her, Miami allowed herself a moment of introspection. For now, the chaos could wait—this was her moment to breathe, surrounded by the kind

of opulence only Yasmeen could deliver.
Many Hours Later, in Moscow

The jet's engines roared while Miami descended the steps into the biting Russian winter. She pulled her plush beige Versace mink coat tighter around her, the chill piercing through the luxurious fabric. Her matching fur boots crunched in the snow as she took a deep breath, the icy air filling her lungs.

The pristine landscape stretched out before her, dazzling under the weak sunlight. For a moment, Miami paused, overwhelmed by a rare sense of connection to the earth. She glanced down at the shimmering snow, feeling a pang of guilt.

"How many of Mother Earth's resources have I burned through?" she whispered to herself, a tear slipping down her cheek.

"Miss Miami, Yasmeen is on line one," the flight attendant called, his voice cutting through the stillness.

Without turning, Miami raised a hand dismissively. "Tell her I'm having a moment." She closed her eyes, focusing on her breath. The pure, crisp air grounded her, filling her with unexpected calm.

The attendant hesitated but obeyed. "Miss Yasmeen, she said she'll call you shortly," he stammered, startled by Miami's unusual demeanor.

Still, Miami remained in place, meditating in the icy stillness, bracing herself for whatever awaited her in Moscow.

Yasmeen paused on the other end, her brow furrowed as she noticed the shift in her friend's tone. She glanced at the phone with a cold, killer stare—an intensity sharp enough to melt icicles. While grabbing the phone to respond, her icy gaze softened into a devious smile.

Before Yasmeen could utter, "You're fired," to the new flight attendant,

Miami snatched the phone and interrupted, "Watch your energy, Yasmeen. Please, calm your storm."

Yasmeen chuckled softly, her voice dripping with amusement and mischief. "Only you could calm me down … Mmm, I feel better just hearing your voice. I swear, I almost killed that flight attendant." Miami let out a light laugh. "Hold on," she said quickly. She grabbed a duffle bag stuffed with $125,000 and handed it to the young flight attendant. "Run," she whispered. The man's eyes widened at the cash before he bolted down the tarmac, disappearing from sight.

"Hello?" Yasmeen's voice rang out, sharp with curiosity. "What on earth is going on over there?"

"Yes, my love," Miami replied, her voice laced with excitement and secrecy. "It's turning into quite the adventure."

"I was starting to worry," Yasmeen said with a slight edge. "The U.S. is a long way off, and you've been out of touch for too long."

Miami laughed softly, a glint of mischief in her eyes. "Oh, Yasmeen, you know I thrive in chaos," she said, her lips curling into a sly smile. "Besides, everything's under control now. The attendant's probably halfway across the city by now."

On the other end of the line, Yasmeen sighed, the sound rich with amusement and exasperation. "You and your little escapades," she muttered. "Miami, your bag with the $125,000 is safely with the rest of your luggage. You know I don't let things slip through my fingers," Yasmeen added, her voice a mix of reassurance and veiled menace. "Don't worry—I won't kill him."

Miami's heart skipped a beat, a flicker of tension gripping her. She wasn't one to take threats lightly, even if they came from Yasmeen. Though the thought of Yasmeen's unpredictable cruelty crossed her mind, deep down, she knew one thing: Yasmeen's loyalty ran deeper than any threat she could issue. Still, the idea of Yasmeen wielding her power made Miami's blood run cold.

"Hello? Did I lose you?" Yasmeen's voice interrupted her thoughts.

Miami shook herself from her reverie. "No, I'm still here," she said, her tone steadying. "So, what's next?" she asked, her voice softer but tinged with curiosity.

"Meet me at the usual spot," Yasmeen replied smoothly. "Your driver will arrive shortly. Take your time—I've got a few things to handle first."

Miami nodded, even though Yasmeen couldn't see her. Reflecting on her eerie confidence, she chuckled lightly. "Perfect," she replied. "I'll be there. Be safe until then, my fierce accomplice."

Yasmeen didn't reply. Instead, the call ended abruptly, leaving Miami to stare at her phone. She chuckled to herself. "Of course, she's too busy to say goodbye," she muttered, sliding her phone into her coat pocket.

Back in Yasmeen's Suite

Yasmeen set her phone down and turned to face the young, terrified flight attendant strapped to a chair in the dimly lit room. Sam's face was pale, his eyes wide with a mixture of fear and pleading. Yasmeen approached him slowly, her heels clicking on the marble floor like a countdown. Her perfectly tailored black pantsuit hugged her figure, and the sparkle of diamond cuffs on her sleeves caught the faint light.

"Sam, sweetheart," Yasmeen purred, her voice dripping with mock affection. "You're quite fortunate, you know. We don't usually offer lessons in survival, but consider today your complimentary education."

Sam stammered, his voice trembling. "I-I didn't mean to—"

"Shh," Yasmeen interrupted, holding a finger to her lips as if quieting a child. She circled him like a predator, her sharp eyes taking in every detail of his trembling form. Her massive Russian bodyguard loomed behind him, his thick hands gripping the chair's backrest.

"How old are you, darling?" Yasmeen asked casually, as if making small talk over tea.

"I'm t-twenty-two," Sam managed, his voice barely above a whisper.

"Twenty-two," Yasmeen repeated, savoring the words like a fine wine. "Ah, such a perfect age to learn life's harsher truths." She leaned closer, her tone dropping to a dangerous murmur. "Strength lies in acceptance, my dear Sam."

Sam's breath hitched, and Yasmeen's sharp nose caught the unmistakable scent of fear—fresh urine pooling beneath him. Yasmeen tilted her head back and let out a sharp, ringing laugh, her amusement both unnerving and genuine.

"Clean him up," Yasmeen barked, waving a dismissive hand at her guard. The man complied, unstrapping Sam and pulling him roughly to his feet.

Before he could leave, Yasmeen grabbed the cigar cutter from the table, snapping it shut in front of Sam's horrified face. The sharp, metallic sound echoed in the room like a gunshot.

"Make sure he gets half the money Miami offered him," Yasmeen ordered coldly. "All in Russian currency."

The bodyguard nodded, dragging the young man toward the door. Sam's legs nearly buckled, but he stumbled forward under the guard's forceful grip.

While the door slammed shut, Yasmeen smoothed her hair and turned back to her glass of wine. "Weakness is such a bore," she muttered to herself, settling back into her armchair.

Fifteen Minutes Later, Inside the Maybach

Miami leaned back in the plush leather seat of Yasmeen's customized Mercedes-Benz Maybach S-Class. The car was a masterpiece of modern luxury, its pearl white exterior glinting under the city lights. Inside, every surface was a symphony of opulence—quilted leather seats with gold stitching, ambient lighting that shifted hues at the touch of a button, and deep ebony wood panels that exuded elegance.

The car's state-of-the-art sound system hummed softly with a playlist of curated classics. "Do you have any Britney Spears? 'Lucky,' specifically," Miami asked, leaning forward with a playful grin.

The driver glanced at her in the rearview mirror, his sharp jawline catching the soft light of the cabin. A faint, seductive smirk curled his lips as he reached for the controls. Moments later, the familiar opening chords of "Lucky" filled the air.

"Ahhh! That's my jam!" Miami exclaimed, throwing her hands up in mock celebration. She leaned back into the leather, the music lifting her spirits as the car glided effortlessly through the streets.

The Maybach purred like a contented lion, its luxurious suspension making every bump on the road vanish. As they cruised through the city, Miami let herself relax for a moment, the soft leather cradling her body and Britney's voice carrying her thoughts far from the chaos that awaited.

This is a story about a girl named Lucky

Early morning, she wakes up
Knock, knock, knock on the door
It's time for makeup, perfect smile
It's you they're all waiting for

They go, "Isn't she lovely, this Hollywood girl?"

And they say
"She's so lucky, she's a star"

But she cry, cry, cries in her lonely heart, thinking,
If there's nothing missing in my life,
Then why do these tears come at night?

Lost in an image, in a dream,
But there's no one there to wake her up
And the world is spinning, and she keeps on winning
But tell me, what happens when it stops?

They go, "Isn't she lovely, this Hollywood girl?"
And they say

The mysterious limo driver stole a glance at Miami through the rearview mirror. She was dancing freely, her fiery red hair bouncing in sync with her movements. Her lips moved to the beat of Britney Spears's "Lucky," and her radiant smile illuminated the dimly lit luxury cabin. The sight was enough to stir something primal in him, his breath hitching as a wave of desire flashed through his mind. He quickly dismissed the thought, tightening his grip on the wheel as he refocused on the icy Moscow roads.

Suddenly, the familiar ring, ring of Miami's phone shattered the moment. She glanced down at the screen of her burner phone, her brows furrowing at the familiar number.

"Hey!" she said, leaning forward and catching the driver's eyes in the mirror. "Can you turn the volume down a little?" Her gaze lingered, daring and unbroken, as though testing his composure.

The driver didn't respond verbally; instead, he pressed a button on the steering wheel. The Maybach's state-of-the-art sound system obeyed instantly, the cabin falling into a serene silence. Miami gave him a curt, approving nod and answered the phone.

"Hello?" she said, her voice steady and cautious.

"Girl, what are you doing?" Paris's energetic voice exploded from the other end of the line.

Miami smirked, leaning back against the plush leather. "I just landed in Thailand," she lied effortlessly, a small grin playing on her lips. She didn't bother questioning how Paris had the number; she knew her friend's tech skills bordered on terrifying.

"Well," Paris said, practically bouncing with excitement, "@ thebloodthatheals is on Instagram Live right now, talking about fruit versus vegetables. It's getting spicy!"

"Can you record it for me?" Miami asked, glancing out the tinted window at the snow-covered streets of Moscow.

"Of course. And FYI," Paris added with a sly chuckle, "I know you're not in Thailand. TTYL." She hung up before Miami could respond.

Miami sighed, her amusement mingling with a sense of unease. Paris's perception was razor-sharp, and it always left Miami feeling exposed. Her gaze drifted to the falling snow outside, her thoughts swirling. She hadn't even processed the chaotic events that had unfolded recently, and now Yasmeen was waiting for her. Would their meeting be a moment of reconciliation—or a violent reckoning?

Her fingers tightened around the lapels of her fur coat while she whispered to herself, "Expect the unexpected."

"I am unstoppable. I am divinely guided, infinitely powerful, and fearlessly aligned with my highest purpose. Everything I desire is already mine."
—Paris D.

Chapter 2

BACK AT THE SAFE HOUSE

in the United States

"You didn't bury it. You just dug the grave, got tired, and left it uncovered. Keep it real."

— Paris

"OUUUUCH!" Samantha screamed as Tokyo ripped the duct tape from her mouth with deliberate cruelty. "What is wrong with you?" she snapped, her voice hoarse from hours of silence. She coughed and spat, the lingering taste of the filthy gym socks that Fatima had stuffed in her mouth days ago!!! "Will you at least give me some water?" she begged, her voice cracking while she wiped her mouth on her shoulder.

Tokyo smirked, grabbing her blowtorch and using the heat to burn through the ropes binding Samantha's arms and legs. She left one arm and leg tied, ensuring Samantha wouldn't think about escaping.

"Here," Tokyo said, handing her a glass of ice water. "I'm amazed you're still alive after enduring those socks."

Samantha snatched the water greedily, gulping it down while eyeing Tokyo warily. "Why are you being so nice?"

"Hold on!" Tokyo snapped, snatching the glass back before Samantha could finish. "We need to talk."

"What do you want from me?" Samantha asked, her heart pounding.

Tokyo leaned in close, her eyes cold and calculating. "Something's different about you. Your energy's softer—more forgiving. Did that bullet to the head change something?" She grabbed Samantha's chin roughly, examining the infected wound on her forehead. "This looks bad," she muttered. "We need to clean it before it kills you."

"It's just a scratch," Samantha spat.

Tokyo shook her head. "It's not just a scratch if it leaves you vulnerable." Without warning, she smacked Samantha with the unlit blowtorch, the metal striking with a dull thud.

Samantha let out a pained scream, her body jerking in the chair. Before she could say more, Tokyo pulled a syringe from her pocket, injecting the tranquilizer fluid into Samantha's neck. Samantha's body slackened instantly, her head lolling to the side.

"Nighty-night," Tokyo whispered, patting her on the head like a child. She straightened and walked away casually. "I should catch up on some anime," she muttered, leaving Samantha unconscious in the dimly lit room.

Back in Moscow, Russia

The heavy wooden doors to Yasmeen's sprawling Russian estate creaked open, revealing the grand opulence of the mansion. Miami stepped inside, her boots clicking softly on the polished floors as her breath formed misty clouds in the freezing air.

Suddenly, a figure swung down from the fourth floor, descending gracefully on a thick rope. Yasmeen let go in midair, performing a flawless backflip before landing on the marble floor with the elegance of a gymnast.

Miami froze, her green eyes wide in admiration. "So, have you joined the circus?" she teased, masking her awe with humor.

Yasmeen strode toward her, her movements like liquid silk. Her long black hair flowed behind her, and her striking green eyes shimmered like emeralds. The caramel hue of her flawless skin seemed to glow in the dim light room. To anyone else, Yasmeen looked like a goddess, but Miami saw the truth: The souls of the damned followed her, trailing behind her in a grotesque, unseen procession.

"Before you come any closer," Miami said, pulling her fur coat tighter around her chest, her green eyes narrowing. "Can you call off your army of lost souls?"

Yasmeen froze mid-step, her sharp gaze locking onto Miami. The air between them felt heavy, charged with unspoken tension. Without breaking eye contact, Yasmeen raised her hands and clapped three times. Instantly, the eerie presence of the lost souls evaporated, the temperature in the room rising slightly as their oppressive energy dissipated.

"Better," Miami muttered, her voice laced with sarcasm and defiance.

Yasmeen's lips curled into a slow, predatory smile. Her voice, low and intoxicating, wrapped around Miami like a spell. "Come here."

Miami hesitated, her body betraying her mind while an invisible force seemed to pull her forward. Despite her inner warnings, she stepped closer, drawn into Yasmeen's orbit like a moth to a flame. The moment their lips met, an electric current surged through her, igniting a tempest of emotions she could no longer control.

The kiss deepened, their movements synchronized as though choreographed by an unseen force. Thunder roared outside, shaking the ground beneath them. Lightning flashed, illuminating the ornate room in bursts of blinding white. Yasmeen's hands moved to Miami's fur coat, sliding it off her shoulders in a single fluid motion.

Miami gasped, her breath hitching as Yasmeen's touch sent shockwaves through her body. A heat unlike anything she had ever felt began to swell within her, radiating outward. The air became stifling, thick with a power neither of them fully understood. Miami's feet lifted off the ground, her body floating weightlessly as if tethered to Yasmeen by some magnetic pull.

Yasmeen's smirk deepened, her voice teasing. "Mmm, seems like you've learned to control that, too."

But Miami wasn't in control. Her body, her mind—everything felt as if it belonged to Yasmeen now. A storm raged inside her, mirroring the one outside, while she surrendered to the unrelenting power Yasmeen had unleashed.

"Why are you doing this?" Miami demanded, her voice trembling as she finally broke free of the trance. Her chest heaved with the effort of regaining composure.

Yasmeen didn't respond immediately. Her silence was sharp, cutting deeper than any words could.

"I would've given you everything!" Miami's voice cracked with desperation, the vulnerability in her tone betraying her anger.

At last, Yasmeen spoke, her lips curling into a sly, calculated smile. "What's the fun in that?" she replied, her tone dripping with mockery.

She took a deliberate step forward, the sound of her heels clicking against the marble floor echoing in the vast space. Her $1.3 million Christian Louboutin heels, adorned with encrusted rubies, shimmering diamonds, and sharp, deadly spikes, gleamed in the lightning flashes.

Each step was a display of power, a reminder of her dominance.

Miami closed her eyes, her breaths slowing as she centered herself. She began to hum softly, her voice carrying a melody ancient and raw, steeped in wisdom beyond human comprehension. Entering a deep state of meditation, she connected to the source of love within her, focusing all her energy on her heart chakra. Her humming grew louder, resonating with a frequency that shook the very foundations of the estate.

Suddenly, a brilliant light erupted from her chest, flooding the room with a golden radiance. The glow illuminated every shadowed corner, pushing back the darkness with an intensity that felt otherworldly.

Yasmeen froze mid-stride, her confident smirk replaced by a flicker of unease. "What is that power?" she whispered, her voice barely audible. Her eyes widened, a mix of awe and fury crossing her face.

The light expanded, engulfing Yasmeen entirely. She staggered, her body no longer obeying her. "What … what is this?" she screamed, her voice cracking as she struggled against the invisible force restraining her.

Miami stood firm, tears streaming down her face. "I would've given you my love. Why would you betray me like this?" she murmured, her voice breaking while the ache in her heart radiated outward.

The golden light surged, growing brighter and more overwhelming. Yasmeen's confidence crumbled, her dominance melting away as the balance of power shifted. Miami's chant resonated through the room, a hauntingly beautiful melody that held the weight of centuries.

Yasmeen let out one final scream before collapsing to her knees, her head bowed as the radiant energy consumed her. Miami stood above her, no longer trembling but resolute, her heartbreak transformed into an unyielding strength.

"Close your eyes and breathe deeply. Feel the energy of the universe flowing through you, filling every part of your being with light and warmth. You are not separate from the world around you—you are a vital part of it, as infinite and radiant as the stars."
—Paris D.

Chapter 3
SAVE THE OCEAN
in the United States

We have to stop polluting our oceans!

Miami jolted awake, gasping. *What the f*** just happened? Was that a dream? It felt so real!*

Her thoughts were interrupted by the handsome limousine driver.

"Are you all right, Miss?" NAS asked, his deep voice smooth and steady.

"Yeah, I'm fine. Where are we? Why aren't we moving?"

"We hit a bad winter storm. The wrecker's on its way—should be about twenty more minutes. Would you like a drink while we wait?" NAS asked, his tone laced with subtle seduction.

"Sure. Make it strong," Miami replied, letting out a relieved sigh.

While, NAS prepared her drink, his phone rang. "Excuse me," he said, answering the call while he stepped out of the luxurious Maybach AMG.

Watching him leave, Miami felt a pang of suspicion. *Why does he need so much privacy?* she wondered, her unease growing.

"Did you do it yet?" Yasmeen asked with a cold yet resolved voice. "Boss, that could kill her! I thought you wanted her alive!"

"No more questions. Do what I say, or I'll head downstairs and have some fun with your wife," Yasmeen threatened, holding a knife to NAS's wife's throat.

NAS clenched his fists, saying nothing. He glanced back at the Maybach, knowing there was no other choice.

"10-4," he muttered, guilt and resentment heavy in his voice.

The line disconnected with a cold click. NAS stared at the setting sun, Moscow's icy wind biting at his face. *How did I end up here? Where did it all go wrong?*

The phone rang again, shattering his thoughts.

"NAS speaking."

"Good evening. My name is Alex. I'm with Maybach Roadside Assistance," said the voice on the other end.

"Listening," NAS replied curtly.

"The ETA is just over twenty minutes. We've run into a small issue, but rest assured, we'll have you out in no time."

NAS ended the call without another word, glancing toward the backseat while Miami appeared deep in thought.

Who is he talking to? Miami wondered, already formulating a plan.

Ring!

"Hello?" Miami answered.

"Are you okay?" Paris asked, her tone full of concern.

"Yes, I'm fine," Miami lied smoothly.

"Listen, I'm having a bit of a problem," Paris began.

"Paris, can't this wait?" Miami asked, slipping off her boots.

"Have you checked Instagram lately? The world's gone crazy!" Paris pressed.

"No, but I'm sure you're about to tell me," Miami sighed.

"All the Nike stores are getting robbed left and right! These people are wiping them clean in one hit!"

"What? That doesn't even make sense. They'd need an army, and where are the cops?" Miami said while unbuttoning her high-waisted ALAÏA jeans.

"Exactly my point! Are you sure you're okay? My spirit tells me you're sitting in the back of a Maybach, undressing," Paris said suspiciously.

"I'm getting ready to meet someone," Miami lied again, sliding off her Victoria's Secret lingerie.

"Here's my suggestion," Paris said slyly. "Stay naked, but throw that fur coat back on. Trust me."

"Paris, it's like you're right here next to me with those psychic gifts of yours," Miami chuckled.

"TTYL. We'll talk more about this Nike situation later, but I think you've got bigger fish to fry. Respectfully," Paris said before ending the call.

Miami hung up just as the back door of the Maybach opened.

"You like what you see?" Miami asked seductively, ignoring the winter cold that nipped at her Flower.

"Let me warm those lips… down there… with my lips," he suggested boldly.

"Get in. I got something better to show you!"

Nas immediately closed the back door while unloosening his tie. His eyes locked onto the beautiful and rare sight of Miami. His manhood began to grow in his slacks. Miami stopped and gave him an intense stare while checking out his manhood.

Damn! I gotta give it to the driver—his body, face, skin, teeth, hair, and his manhood came from pure stardust! He is everything a woman needs! she said to herself while he stripped and came much closer.

Damn, even his breath smells heavenly! she thought.

"You smell good too," he said while he gently squeezed her nipples.

"Hmm… listen—as much as I like this foreplay, we don't have much time, so let's get straight to it," Miami said, signaling that she wanted to get on top.

"You're a woman who knows what she wants. I like that," he said, while watching Miami straddle him.

"Mmmm…" they both moaned when he entered.

His eyes began to roll in the back of his head while Miami used him like the puppet he was.

"I'm—cum…" Before he could finish, Miami immediately slit his throat with one quick, disrespectful slice. Blood squirted all over Miami's body as the tow truck approached.

"Okay, Miami, think!" she said while reaching for the wet wipes inside her purse.

While she cleaned the blood off her face and hands, she quickly put on her fur coat and boots, admiring the beautiful man she had just slaughtered.

Omg, I gotta get rid of this roadside assistance agent! Miami said while exiting the luxurious 2025 Maybach.

"Hello, miss. I'm Alex, Maybach Roadside Assistance. Where is Nas?" he asked, examining the car.

"Nas left to the nearest store to get me some personal items—it's that time of the month," she lied while eyeing Alex.

He looks just like Nas… are they related? she thought, quickly shaking off the thought.

"Hey, it's cold! How long will this take?" she asked, pulling her Versace fur coat tighter against her naked skin.

Why in the heck didn't I at least put on panties? she chuckled silently. "Alex!" she yelled. "Snap out of it!"

"So sorry… I was just in a daze. You're so beautiful, miss."

"Give me like 15 minutes," he said with a strong Russian accent.

15 minutes later

"Have a good evening, miss. If you need anything, don't hesitate to call me," said Alex while he drove off.

"Thank you so much," Miami said, now seated in the driver's seat of the Maybach.

Whew, that was close. Okay, now I gotta blow this mother up!

Maybe coming to Russia was a bad idea. Seems I've lost my damn mind completely too. I wonder if there's a new virus going around…

When she settled into the driver's seat, her mind raced.

What if Alex is working for Yasmeen? she thought, while glancing in the rearview mirror.

Then it hit her—she had forgotten Nas' dead body was still in the back seat.

She realized the dire predicament she was in and knew she had to act fast.

Carefully steering the Maybach through the dimly lit roads of Moscow, Miami scanned the surroundings. Her heart was pounding.

She spotted an old industrial area down a side street.

I wonder if that warehouse is empty? she thought, making a quick right into the complex.

The rusty gates creaked open while the Maybach rolled into the abandoned warehouse yard. She parked and opened the door cautiously, the cold air sending shivers through her. She tiptoed into the shadows, senses sharp, ears tuned for any sound.

Suddenly—a noise.

"What was that?" she asked, flashing her light toward the sound.

Caught off guard, she tensed.

Okay, Miami. Calm down—it's just a raccoon. Omg… raccoons… that brings back so many memories, she thought, refocusing on the task at hand.

She maneuvered around the curious raccoon, making a mental note to investigate later.

Damn, this body is extremely heavy! she thought, pulling Nas' cold body out of the backseat.

Feeling the weight of the body, she struggled to drag it deeper into the shadows of the warehouse.

Just a few more feet, she thought, while her heart pounded!

Exhausted, she finally managed to conceal the body. But the weight of what she had done settled heavily on her shoulders.

Is this the consequences of my actions? Miami wondered, the realization of her path crashing in.

Suddenly, distant sirens pierced the night, sending a chill through her spine.

With panic flooding her, she frantically searched for a way out.

This alley is a labyrinth… The walls suddenly felt like they were closing in.

Sweat formed on her brow as she weighed her options.

Should I climb the fence or try that narrow, dark pass?

She made a split-second decision—she dashed toward the fence, adrenaline in her veins. She reached the top, flung herself over, and hit the ground hard. Pain surged through her, but she pushed through it.

That wasn't the police. I know that was Yasmeen Gones! she thought, grabbing her phone.

She quickly texted her closest ally, detailing everything and urging them to meet her at a safe location.

While she walked through the snow, her phone buzzed. The message read: *Meet me at the abandoned warehouse on Rue de Lune. I'll send a helicopter. It'll take you to a private airstrip. Send me your location!*

With a deep breath, Miami felt a flicker of relief.

10 minutes later

A helicopter approached, blades cutting through the freezing air. The whirlwind of snow and dust created a perfect whiteout.

Perfect cover, she whispered as she entered the helicopter unseen.

Inside, she buckled up, her heart still racing. The chopper lifted off into the night sky. Below, Moscow twinkled—breathtaking and distant.

She leaned back, looking out the window, the city lights glowing beneath her.

That raccoon… it sparked an old memory from her college days!! She had always been drawn to the enigmatic creature, with its clever eyes and mischievous nature. After all these years, the sight of a raccoon still held a special place in Miami's heart.

She was transported back—
To campus.
To a night.

To a bold and cunning raccoon that stole her keys, leading her on a wild chase across the quad.

That memory never left her.

Flashback: 2017 — Alabama A&M College Party

The music was already blaring inside the old warehouse when Sarah, the de facto ringleader of the group, triumphantly held up the keys to their makeshift venue.

"All right, ladies and gentlemen," Sarah announced with a smug grin, "we're about to make history tonight!"

The girls cheered, their excitement echoing in the empty parking lot. Miami stood at the back, arms crossed, a knowing smirk tugging at her lips.

"Who'd you have to screw to pull this off?" Akemi asked, her voice dripping with mockery.

"No, no," Mocha interjected with a sly grin. "The real question is: How many?"

The group erupted in laughter, their voices blending with the bass thumping from inside. Miami rolled her eyes, brushing past the girls and heading toward the stage area. She had no time for their childish antics.

"You know, Miami," Mocha called after her, her tone biting, "for someone who thinks she's above us, you sure love to boss people around!"

Miami stopped mid-stride, turning with a sharp glare. "Mocha, if your game was as strong as your mouth, maybe you'd have brought a DJ who showed up on time. Now, excuse me—I have money to make."

Mocha lunged, her temper flaring, but Sarah and Akemi quickly held her back. "Let me go!" Mocha yelled. "Y'all always saving her!"

Ignoring the drama, Miami pulled out her phone and dialed a number, speaking rapidly in Spanish. Her words were sharp and commanding, arranging for a replacement DJ to be at the warehouse in under thirty minutes.

Twenty-five minutes later, the sound of engines rumbled in the distance. Miami's lips curled into a triumphant smile as three sleek black vans pulled up to the warehouse entrance.

"You see those vans?" Akemi asked, her voice full of awe.

Mocha's mouth hung open. "Wait, is that—?"

Miami didn't wait for their reactions. She jogged toward the lead van, her heels clicking against the asphalt. As the doors opened, one of the hottest DJs in the city stepped out, his entourage trailing behind him.

"DJ Vibez," Miami greeted him with a confident nod, "glad you could make it."

He smirked, looking her up and down. "You got the payment?"

Miami handed him a fat envelope. "All here. Now, let's turn this place up."

Back in the Present

Miami jolted awake while the helicopter hit turbulence, snapping her out of the memory. She glanced at her phone, rereading the message from her ally: *Meet me at the abandoned warehouse on Rue de Lune.*

As the helicopter began its descent, Miami felt a renewed determination. That college party had been her first taste of power—proving she could command respect, outmaneuver her competition, and get what she wanted at any cost.

And now, in the snow-covered streets of Moscow, she would prove it again.

The Flashback Continues:

Miami continued to let her memories drift back to her college days—it was her safe space, a refuge from the chaos of her present reality.

"Ohhh, thank you so much, DJ Vibez!" Miami yelled, throwing her arms around him in a tight hug, her excitement evident as she planted a kiss on his cheek.

Miami always had the hottest celebs and DJs in her back pocket.

"Thanks for coming! This means so much to us!" Miami gushed, bouncing on her toes with excitement.

"You know I wasn't about to let you throw a party without me," DJ Vibez said, flashing his diamond-studded smile. "Plus, I'd do anything for you, baby girl. Now, let's get this party started."

He winked, turning to his crew and directing them to set up the equipment. As the anticipation grew, music filled the air, and the warehouse transformed into a dazzling party venue.

But beneath the glitz and excitement of the night, Miami harbored a brewing storm.

The Night Before the Party

"Oh, they think they're slick? They think they can get away with this?" Miami muttered to herself, gripping the steering wheel tightly. Her mind raced with suspicion as she thought about Mocha and DJ Valentino.

"Just how long has this been going on?" she asked herself, taking a puff of her cannabis to calm her nerves.

Miami's instincts were rarely wrong, and the way Mocha and Valentino exchanged sly glances made her stomach churn. She decided to confront them, setting her plan in motion.

The Confrontation

Miami hid in the cramped closet of Valentino's mother's house, her heart pounding in her chest while she waited for her suspicions to be confirmed. Minutes later, the front door creaked open, and laughter filled the house.

"Take me upstairs, bae," Mocha's voice purred.

Miami's blood boiled as she listened to their flirtatious exchanges. Minutes stretched into what felt like hours as she sat in silence, her fists clenched in the darkness of the smelly closet.

Liars, she thought bitterly, tears streaming down her face.

The Next Day

Miami approached Valentino's house, a storm brewing in her chest. Her lips curled into a determined smirk as she adjusted her diamond-studded bra.

Ring! Ring!

"I know you're home," Miami said, her tone sharp and unwavering.

The door opened to reveal Valentino, his 6'5" frame leaning against the doorframe.

"What's good, ma? Why didn't you call?" he asked, his gray eyes sparkling despite the late hour.

"Sorry, baby. My phone died," Miami replied, pushing past him into the house.

Valentino followed her, his gaze lingering on her figure. "Damn, you look good, ma. You smell sweet, too. What's that scent?"

"Lick Me All Over," Miami said with a coy smile. "It's my favorite."

She played along, teasing him with a seductive grin, but her true intentions simmered beneath the surface.

The Trap

Miami mixed their drinks, adding a special ingredient to Valentino's. The sweet scent of Patron masked the bitterness of the powder she'd slipped into his glass.

"To the best head ever!" Miami toasted, raising her glass with a bright smile.

"To you, ma," Valentino replied, lifting his drink and taking a long sip.

Moments later, his expression shifted. "Yo … What's this taste?" he slurred, his movements growing sluggish.

"Shhh," Miami whispered, climbing onto the bed and distracting him with her infamous tongue trick.

As Valentino faded into unconsciousness, Miami's smirk widened. "Game over," she whispered.

The Revenge

Miami wasted no time. She retrieved her Girl Scout knife, her heart racing with adrenaline. In the garage, she sabotaged Valentino's prized DJ equipment, slicing wires and leaving no trace.

But her revenge wasn't complete. From the backseat of her car, she retrieved a cage holding an agitated raccoon. Carefully, she injected the animal with a syringe containing a diluted rabies virus.

"This is going to be good," Miami muttered, opening the cage and releasing the raccoon into the garage. Chaos erupted as the animal darted around, knocking over equipment and creating a deafening commotion.

Miami hurried back upstairs, collected the shot glasses, and destroyed any evidence linking her to the scene. Before leaving, she slashed Valentino's car tires, ensuring he wouldn't chase after her.

While she drove away, her laughter echoed in the silence of the night. "I win. You lose," she whispered triumphantly.

43

44

Chapter 4

THE CHOSEN ONES

The Truth in the Shadows

Autumn's Awakening

Autumn stirred from what felt like an eternity of torment, her body heavy and unresponsive. Shadows danced across the room as she blinked, trying to make sense of her surroundings.

"Where am I? Why can't I move?" she whispered, panic rising in her chest.

A gentle voice echoed in her mind, soothing her fears. It was familiar, yet she couldn't place it.

Fragments of memories flooded her mind—ancient ruins, towering mountains, and a haunting melody. She clung to the images, desperate for clarity.

Suddenly, a shadow emerged from the corner of the room, stepping into the moonlight.

"Hello, Autumn. Don't be afraid, but be afraid!" said the mysterious voice.

Autumn's mind struggled to focus, her body sluggish from the heavy sedation. Her surroundings were a blur, disorienting, and she found it hard to grasp what was happening.

"You will know the truth soon, my dear," the voice continued, cold and cryptic, right before a sharp prick at her arm. The figure injected a high dose of morphine into her IV.

Her eyelids grew heavy while the drug coursed through her veins, pulling her into a thick fog. The world around her faded into an indistinct blur. The voice leaned closer, whispering, "The truth will set you free," before fading into the shadows, leaving Autumn to drift into unconsciousness.

Back @ Safe House
Location: Kennesaw, GA

"Okay! Now, what is going on?" Tokyo asked in confusion, frustration rising in her voice.

"Why isn't anyone picking up their phones?" The uneasy silence that followed Tokyo's words seemed to seep into every corner of the safe house, heightening the tension. The unanswered calls only deepened the unsettling atmosphere. Tokyo couldn't shake the feeling that something was terribly wrong, and she needed answers—fast.

"I need to leave this safe house. Where is Miami, and why isn't anyone picking up? I'm getting a really bad feeling!" Tokyo said while frantically checking her emails, hoping for any sign of progress. The silence persisted, only making her feel more isolated. Something deeper was at play, and she knew she couldn't ignore it.

Ring ... Ring ... The phone on the desk suddenly rang, breaking through the tension.

"Tokyo, what's up?" came Carter's voice from the other end.

"I'm glad you reached back out!" Tokyo replied, relief washing over her.

"I'm here to help, Tok. What's going on?" Carter's voice remained steady, though concern clearly lingered beneath the surface.

"You know I'm babysitting Operation *City Girl Down,*" Tokyo replied, throwing a pointed look of death toward Samantha.

"Okay. Let me give you a brief update," Carter said, his voice serious. "Miami is on the way to a safe house in Paris. Zeke's in lockup, and Kena's MIA in Dubai. We've got people looking for her, but we should hear from her soon."

Tokyo nodded, focusing on Carter's briefing while she tried to calm the storm brewing inside her.

"This world is run by some sick people," Carter continued, pausing briefly to take a hit of the finest cannabis Paris had to offer. "My team recovered bodies from the old water house on the west side of Atlanta."

Tokyo's stomach turned at the thought. She could already sense where this was heading.

"The identities trace back to some government officials," Carter added, making himself more comfortable in his plush leather office chair.

"Can you explain the goat heads?" Tokyo asked, her mind whirring with possibilities. She had to know everything now, every detail.

Carter leaned forward, exhaling a puff of smoke. "Well, the goat heads were real. Somehow, these sick individuals created masks out of actual goat heads."

"These guys bought goats just to kill them and make masks?" Tokyo asked, her voice almost incredulous.

"Yes, they actually used real goat heads. It's beyond disturbing," Carter said while flipping through his case files.

Tokyo's eyes widened in disbelief, and she felt the weight of the situation pressing on her. "See? I knew something wasn't right." She took a deep breath, trying to steady her nerves.

BOOM! BOOM! The explosions rocked the safe house, and before Tokyo could react, the phone slipped from her hands. Blood trickled down her soft, caramel skin while she lay on the bed, vision blurring while she struggled to stay conscious.

Carter jumped from his chair, heart pounding in his chest. "Tokyo! Stay with me, Tokyo! Just hold on; help is on the way!"

But Tokyo's body lay lifeless, the phone now silent. The sound of the shots had told Carter everything he needed to know. He didn't have to assume anything—years of living in a world of violence had already prepared him for this. Tokyo was gone.

Samantha's Betrayal

The mysterious woman quickly ended the call and destroyed Tokyo's SIM card. Then, with cold precision, she smashed the phone against the ground of the old safe house.

With Tokyo out of the way, Samantha meticulously checked the room to make sure there were no other forms of communication left behind. "Let's stay on track. I have to find Autumn," she muttered to herself, her mind laser-focused on the task at hand.

She exited the front door, intent on carrying out the next part of her plan.

Carter's Resolve

Back on the other end, Carter had already begun making arrangements.

"I need you to head to this location," he instructed.

"Got it, boss," Blue responded quickly. "I'll let you know once it's done."

Carter's voice was sharp. "This time, don't dispose of the body. I want it delivered to NovaGaia Cemetery in Dunwoody, Georgia."

Blue didn't hesitate. "Understood. I'll take care of it."

The Call from Mrs. Beretta

Just as Carter was deep in thought, his phone buzzed once more. He saw it was a call from Miss Beretta, and his pulse quickened.

With a resigned sigh, he answered. "Carter, baby," came her sharp, cold voice.

"Yes, Mrs. B," Carter replied.

"What's the status?" Her tone was commanding, sharp as ever.

"We're making progress," Carter said, keeping his voice steady despite the weight of the situation.

"I want Samantha's head delivered to my doorstep, baby!" Mrs. Beretta demanded, her voice icily determined.

"Mrs. B, you're pushing ninety. Put that eagle away. I'm on it," Carter replied, attempting to lighten the mood, though it fell flat.

"I'm eighty-two, and I could still outshoot you any day. It's just my knees aren't what they used to be," Mrs. Beretta responded with a wry smile in her voice.

Carter chuckled. "I'll take care of it. It's a very delicate situation."

"Not as delicate as my poor, beautiful granddaughter, Tokyo, who's on her way to NovaGaia Cemetery," Mrs. Beretta's voice cracked with grief. "Oh, you thought I didn't know, huh?"

Carter fell silent. He knew she never missed a thing.

"That's right, and I know a few things about Samantha, too. Now, you know I'm retired, but Carter, if this isn't handled in forty-eight hours, I'm coming out of retirement," she said. Then, the unmistakable sound of gunfire echoed as she shot two flies messing with her watermelon patch.

"Mrs. B, are you okay?" Carter asked, his voice laced with concern.

"Yeah, these damn flies are messing with my watermelons," she answered gruffly.

"Did you hit your targets?" Carter asked with a hint of sarcasm.

"I split them into four pieces. It was two flies, by the way!" she said, her tone lightening for a moment. But then, her voice softened. "Tokyo's death … it's broken me. She was my heart."

Carter's heart sank. "I got to go," Mrs. Beretta said before hanging up, her voice thick with emotion.

Carter took a deep breath, but before he could collect himself, his phone buzzed again. This time, it was Tessa.

"What's up, Tessa?" Carter answered, knowing she had important intel.

"Carter! I've got so much intel on *Operation Diddy Bop!*" Tessa's voice was buzzing with excitement as she set up her live stream.

"Send me everything you've got," Carter replied urgently, taking a quick shot of Knob Creek to steady his nerves.

"Will do! Check out my live tonight. Remember, Tessa Tells. Muah! Much love and blessings!" Tessa signed off, leaving Carter to scramble through the overwhelming amount of information.

"Thanks, Tessa. I'll be checking it out," Carter murmured before ending the call.

He opened the files, feeling a sense of dread creeping in while the magnitude of *Operation Diddy Bop* became clearer with every document. The intel was extensive—almost too much to process. Carter leaned back in his chair, allowing the weight of it all to settle in.

"We have to get this right," Carter whispered to himself, his voice laced with urgency. His phone buzzed again.

Carter's Desperation

Carter glanced at his phone and saw it was from Miss Beretta again. His pulse quickened.

"Yes, Mrs. B?" he asked, trying to keep his tone even.

"I've been watching your progress, Carter," Mrs. Beretta said coldly. "You better not let this slide."

"I won't, Mrs. B," Carter replied, determination clear in his voice.

The gravity of Tokyo's death and the upcoming tasks weighed on Carter, but he couldn't afford to falter. "All right, let's get to work," he muttered to himself. The next forty-eight hours would determine everything.

The Secret Journal

Carter sighed deeply. Mrs. Beretta, tough as nails, was visibly shaken by Tokyo's death. Desperation clawed at him while he realized everything was spiraling out of control. He had to get to the truth. Grabbing his coat, Carter stormed out the door, determined to find answers. Snowflakes drifted from the dark sky while he sped through the Paris streets in his all-black unmarked 2025 Mercedes Benz G-Wagon AMG. His mind was clouded, questions swirling around him like the cold wind outside. The flashing city lights blurred while he thought of Tokyo, of her energy, her laughter—now all absent. Her final words haunted him.

He found himself at the old café where Tokyo had often hung out. It was almost empty, the dim lighting casting shadows in the corners. He approached the counter, scanning the few patrons, looking for someone who could help. The barista, a middle-aged man with salt-and-pepper hair, nodded in recognition.

"Bonsoir, Monsieur. What can I get you tonight?"

Carter leaned in close to avoid being overheard. "I need some information," he said, his voice edged with urgency.

"One mocha latte, no sugar, no creamer, coming right up," the barista replied with a nod.

Carter's gaze never left the door, a feeling of being watched tugging at the back of his mind. The barista returned, sliding the drink across the counter. Carter took a cautious sip, his fingers tapping on the worn surface.

"So, who are you looking for?" the barista asked, voice low.

"Elise," Carter replied, eyes scanning the room. "She's vital to my mission. I don't have much time."

The barista raised an eyebrow. "Elise, you say? There's a regular named Elise who comes in once or twice a week, usually in the mornings."

"When was the last time you saw her?" Carter asked, his pinky raised slightly while he sipped the bitter coffee three times.

"Two days ago, I think," the barista replied. "She might come by tomorrow."

Carter nodded. "Merci," he muttered, trying to mask his urgency.

Suddenly, the barista motioned for Carter to follow him. Without hesitation, Carter trailed him down a narrow hallway, the low light casting shadows against the brick walls. They reached a small door at the end of the corridor, and the barista unlocked it, revealing a dimly lit, private room. A faint scent of lavender lingered in the air.

"What is this place?" Carter asked, his curiosity piqued.

"This," the barista said, his voice barely a whisper, "is where secrets are told, and hidden truths come to light."

Carter took a seat at the table. His eyes swept across the room. The door clicked shut behind the barista, and after what felt like an eternity, he returned with a small, ornate box. He placed it gently on the table and sat across from Carter.

"Inside this box," the barista began, "lies the key to a story that has been buried for generations. A story intertwined with this city's very soul."

The barista opened the box slowly, revealing a worn, leather-bound journal.

"The pages within hold the memories of a life lived in the shadows of Paris. The truths are buried deep—protected by a secret society that has been operating in the dark for centuries."

Carter's hand itched to touch the journal. "Your arrival here, Carter," the barista said, eyes glinting in the dim light, "is no coincidence. You've been chosen to uncover what so many have died protecting."

With a deep breath, Carter reached out, fingers brushing the ancient leather. A shiver ran down his spine. He opened the journal, revealing pages filled with cryptic sketches, maps, and foreign text. The first page displayed an intricate symbol—a gilded fleur-de-lis intertwined with serpents, underscored by a language Carter couldn't decipher.

"Elise is a code name," the barista said, his voice growing more intense. "Only a few know how to find this place at this hour and ask the questions you did. Who taught you our code, young man?"

Carter's heart stopped. "Tokyo," he whispered.

The barista's face went pale. "Tokyo?" he repeated, a hint of disbelief in his voice. "I've been searching for Tokyo. Where is she?"

Carter's pulse quickened. "Tokyo is dead," he said, his voice low. "She was murdered during an operation. We don't know how Samantha escaped. She was bound and gagged."

Tommie, the barista, leaned back in his chair, a troubled look crossing his face. "Maybe the safe house was compromised," he suggested, but Carter didn't have the answer.

"We'll find the answers soon," Carter replied, his tone resolute.

Tommie sighed. "Samantha's not the person she once was. She was our most trusted ally, but now …" He trailed off, his voice heavy with regret. "I always told Tokyo that this life wasn't for her. Hearts may be fragile, but resilience is crucial in our line of work."

Carter's mind raced. "What do you know about Samantha?"

Tommie hesitated before responding. "Let's talk over dinner. I'll need a full stomach and some privacy," he said, guiding Carter out of the private room.

As they stepped into the cold Parisian night, the weight of their mission hung heavy in the air. Their footsteps echoed in the quiet streets while the chill settled into their bones. They walked in silence, Carter's mind racing with questions. It wasn't long before they reached a secluded restaurant tucked away in an alley, the hustle of the city muffled by the walls.

The maître d' greeted them with a nod and led them to a private area at the back. Inside, the atmosphere was drastically different. The room was filled with vintage posters and exposed brick, lit by lanterns that cast an eerie glow. This was no ordinary restaurant.

"This is where we'll talk," Tommie said, leading Carter to a table in the far corner.

While Carter sat down, the weight of what was coming pressed on him. The mysteries surrounding Tokyo's death, the cryptic journal, and Samantha's betrayal—all of it was leading to something bigger. And he was running out of time.

"Let's get to the truth," Carter whispered to himself, his mind steeling for what was to come.

Let's call a cat a cat!!
—Diamond

Chapter 5

SPEAK TO ME, LORD ENKI

Back in Alpharetta, Georgia

Secrets of the Old and New! Anianki

"Where is Miami, and why hasn't she returned any of my calls?" Paris asked, her voice softened while she juiced fresh fruits and vegetables from the mini garden. She paused, taking a moment to appreciate the calmness the house offered. The natural light filtered through the expansive windows, reflecting off the soft tones of the eco-friendly décor. It was the peace she needed, a sanctuary to collect her thoughts before the storm of uncertainty that awaited.

"Miami has been elusive lately," Chief Dixon replied, his voice tinged with concern. "The last we heard, she was following a lead near the old train station in Russia."

Paris's heart tightened. The mention of Russia only deepened the mystery. Miami had always been ahead of the game, so her silence now was deafening. Paris paced, her footsteps silent on the polished hardwood floors, the house exuding an almost ethereal calm. The subtle scent of lavender and eucalyptus from the air diffusers mixed with the soft sound of distant birdsong outside. It was the kind of environment that encouraged peace—but also allowed doubt to grow.

"We need to send someone to check it out," Paris insisted, the urgency

57

in her tone cutting through the calm of her home.

Chief Dixon nodded gravely. "I'll arrange for an operative to investigate immediately." He paused, his eyes scanning Paris's face, reading the worry in her expression. "We will get answers. You're not in this alone."

"I'm headed out to the office. I have to find out more about Operation Mongoose," Chief Dixon said, his frustration palpable.

"We've been chasing that goose for months now," Paris muttered under her breath, running a hand through her hair while her mind continued to race.

"I know we'll have this wrapped up soon," Chief Dixon reassured her, trying to calm the storm brewing inside her.

Paris's expression softened as she turned toward him. "Andre," she called softly, the weight of the world momentarily melting away.

"I like it when you call me Chief," Andre teased, his eyes glimmering with affection while he admired the subtle way the light flickered off Paris's smooth skin.

Her laugh was a soft, fleeting sound that filled the room with warmth, a brief escape from the pressures they both carried. But soon, business returned to the forefront of their minds.

"Back to business," Paris murmured, her smile fading.

"Yes, Paris," he said, his voice filled with compassion. "Always."

The intensity between them was undeniable, but the gravity of the mission loomed large. Still, there was a moment—just a fraction of a second—where everything else fell away. Andre pulled her close, his hands cradling her face, and their kiss deepened. Their lips met with an urgency that spoke of months of pent-up emotion, igniting something that neither of them could ignore. It was electric, the world outside fading to nothing while they lost themselves in the intensity of their connection. The kiss wasn't just a kiss—it was a fusion of hearts and souls, a release that left them breathless and craving more.

Paris's body trembled against his, the warmth of his touch sparking a fire deep within her. Each movement was as natural as it was passionate, their hearts syncing in a rhythm all their own. While they pulled away, the air between them crackled with energy, both reluctant to break the bond they had just formed.

"We can't ignore it," Paris whispered breathlessly, the urgency of their responsibilities cutting through the warmth of the connection they shared.

"I know," Andre replied, though the hesitation in his voice betrayed the tug-of-war between love and duty.

They pulled away slowly, the moment lingering in the air. The peace of the house settled around them again, offering solace for just a moment longer before duty called.

"I have to get to the office. I'll see you when I get home … or maybe at work?" Andre winked, quickly adjusting his uniform pants before rushing out the door.

The sound of the door closing behind him left Paris standing in the quiet, a heavy sigh escaping her lips.

Ring. Ring. Ring.

"Hello?" Paris answered, attempting to stand up from the dining room floor, where she had collapsed moments earlier.

"Are you okay?" Diamond's voice crackled through the phone.

"I'm trying to get up off the floor," Paris said, her laugh light despite the tension of the day.

"P! Why you on the floor, love?" Diamond asked, her voice teasing but concerned.

"Long story short, Chief Dixon had me in handcuffs," Paris laughed, finally managing to stand and wipe her hands on her pants.

"Hmmm, handcuffs? Did he beat it up and catch a charge?" Diamond's voice was playful, but Paris could hear the genuine curiosity underneath.

"We'll follow up later," Paris said with a slight chuckle. "Okay, enjoy your day."

Paris ended the call, feeling the familiar weight of the day press upon her once more. She turned toward the bathroom, grateful for the sanctuary it provided.

The steam in the shower engulfed her, cascading over her body like a gentle embrace. The soothing aroma of eucalyptus drifted through the air, offering her a moment of peace, a brief escape. Each breath she took was calming, filling her with a sense of serenity that she desperately needed. The droplets of water pattered softly on the tiles, a natural symphony that eased her troubled mind. "You're my oasis in this chaos," she whispered to herself, her thoughts drifting to the uncertainty surrounding Miami.

Paris took a deep breath, wiping away the lingering tears as she composed herself. The house—her sanctuary—had offered her peace. She stepped out of the shower and wrapped herself in a soft white silk robe, the fabric gliding against her skin, a reminder of the serenity that she had to hold onto. In front of her full-length mirror, she admired her natural curves, the quiet reflection a reminder of her strength.

"Let's do a light beat," Paris said while she reached for her makeup bag, still located in its usual place beside the stand-up mirror.

She moved methodically, step by step, her movements as deliberate as they were comforting. "First, I'm going to use Fenty Melt Makeup + Nourish with Melt Awf," she said, dabbing the product on her face with care. "Next, let's tone and quench with Fat Water Toner Essence." Her fingers moved with ease while she applied the product, a routine that calmed her nerves. "Last step: Lock N Shield with Hydra Vizor SPF 30, protecting my skin from the harmful sun rays. Now, I'm ready for my day," she said, tapping the final product into her face.

"Hey, Siri," she called, her voice light.

"Umm-hmm?" Siri replied.

"Set a reminder to place an order of Face by Francois. And hair—a twenty-six-inch lace front from D's Hair & Beauty Supply."

"Reminder set," Siri responded.

Paris turned toward the mirror again, her eyes glimmering with determination. While the wind howled outside, Paris dressed quickly, pulling on her coat and stepping into her shoes with purpose. Her platinum blonde hair flowed gracefully behind her, catching the light and casting a soft glow that illuminated her features. Her lips, full and beautifully glossed with Fenty by Rihanna Gloss Bomb, gleamed while they contrasted against the crisp winter air.

With her eyes brimming with determination and a quiet strength emanating from her, Paris held her head high. Despite the uncertainties ahead, she walked with purpose—fierce, unyielding, a force to be reckoned with. The chaos of the world couldn't touch her now, not while she carried the fire of resilience in her soul!

Ring, Ring!

Paris answered, relief washing over her. It was her best friend, Diamond, whom she met in 2013 at an art exhibit in SoHo. "Hey," the familiar voice chimed through, comforting yet urgent.

"Did you get those recent updates on Operation MMJCVITMMB?" Diamond asked, her voice carrying a sense of impending urgency.

"Yes, just received them! We need to act fast," Paris replied, sliding into her pristine 2025 Aston Martin DBX 707. The luxury SUV gleamed in its elegant white finish, exuding a perfect blend of power and sophistication. Inside, the deep red leather bucket seats stood in sharp contrast to the sleek white interior. The futuristic dashboard hummed with cutting-edge technology, giving the impression of a car that had a mind of its own.

At the touch of a button, the 4.0L V8 engine roared to life, sending a surge of power through the car. With 707 horsepower and a top speed of 193 miles per hour, it was ready to move. The vehicle responded with precision, and Paris pressed the accelerator, feeling the car spring forward. The DBX 707's handling was flawless, guiding her toward her off-grid office. The roar of the engine vibrated through the cabin, urging her to push further.

The car responded effortlessly, its suspension absorbing the road's imperfections, making every curve feel like a smooth ride. Paris tightened her grip on the wheel, the luxurious vehicle's sharp agility keeping her mind sharp and focused.

"Girl, let me spill this tea real quick!" Diamond continued, her voice playful but filled with urgency. Paris could almost hear the grin in her tone. "Apparently, there's been a breach. Can you believe it?"

"Pour it!" Paris urged, making a sharp left onto Prosperity Lane. The tires gripped the asphalt without hesitation while the car hugged the road, barely tilting. The smooth suspension kept her grounded, no matter how tight the turn.

"We got new intel that changes everything," Diamond continued, her voice dropping to a conspiratorial whisper. "There's a mole in our midst."

"A mole?" Paris asked, raising an eyebrow, a chuckle escaping her lips. The hint of suspicion crept into her voice. Her fingers tightened on the wheel, the leather smooth under her grip. The vehicle, sensing her urgency, accelerated effortlessly.

"Yes," Diamond replied, her tone now serious. "They've infiltrated deep within the organization."

Paris's mind raced, analyzing the new development. Her eyes narrowed, and she pushed the DBX 707 faster, the engine growling beneath her. The car's speed was exhilarating, and she felt every inch of the road beneath her tires. She focused, knowing the answers she needed were just around the corner.

"Okay, okay, ain't no mole, but girl, some dude is approaching my SUV!! Ahhh!!!" Diamond screamed playfully, her voice laced with excitement. "He's at my window, girl! Hold up, P! Listen, girl!!"

Paris's heart rate spiked, but she kept her eyes fixed on the road, focused on the destination. "What?" she asked, her voice tight with concern.

Diamond's voice cut through the tension. "I like your car," the mysterious man said, leaning casually on her window and flashing a smile. The words hung in the air, their significance only deepening the mystery.

Diamond rolled her eyes but kept her cool. "Thanks. Appreciate it," she replied, her voice smooth despite the underlying tension. Her fingers tapped nervously on the steering wheel.

"You need something?" she asked, irritation edging into her voice.

The man straightened, unfazed by Diamond's cool demeanor. "I might," he replied cryptically, his eyes gleaming with mischief. He handed her a folded piece of paper through the window, their fingers brushing briefly.

Diamond hesitated, eyeing him warily before taking the paper. "I guess we'll see about that," she said, unfolding it cautiously.

Paris's pulse quickened while she imagined the scene. Diamond's voice broke through her thoughts. "It's coordinates—locations I've never heard of before."

"Wait, what? Coordinates?" Paris asked, her mind snapping into focus as she merged onto the highway. The Aston Martin DBX 707 hummed smoothly beneath her once again, the vehicle responding to every command with precision. "Whooo!!! The torque on this thing is unreal!" she screamed while the car surged forward, each push of the pedal feeding her need for speed.

Diamond's nervous laugh echoed in the phone. "I know, right?" she said. "I'm pushing mine right now, too!!"

"I'm gonna follow up on those coordinates," Diamond said, her voice firm. "Momma's calling—I'll hit you right back, P! Don't do anything crazy!"

Paris's grip tightened on the wheel, the engine roaring beneath her. The car responded without hesitation, eager to meet the challenge. She could feel the road stretching out ahead, an invitation to uncover the truth. The winter air cut through the car, but she hardly noticed, lost in the chase.

Tems began to fill the cabin, her voice swelling, amplifying the tension in the car. Paris turned the volume up, letting the music energize her. "Sing, Tems!" she shouted, merging her voice with the singer's. The beats pulsed through the cabin, syncing with the rhythm of the engine, pushing her onward, urging her to stay focused. The answers were waiting, and she was determined to find them.

This is the peace that you cannot buy
Send me a love that you cannot mix
One is the joy that you cannot waste
And the other one price that you cannot fix
This is the peace that you cannot buy
Finding a way, when you cannot see
Man will desist if he cannot pray
I need to find release

[Pre-Chorus]
But behind my mind it runs
All these thoughts of troubling
Fighting to give up my pain
Fighting to be on my lane
My mind running to the other side
When it's time to live my life
Then, it tries to take me out
Tell you what I need right here

I really need, I really need mine now
I really need, I need a free mind now
I really need, I really need time now
I really need, I need to free my mind now
I really need, I really need time now
I really need, I need a free mind now
I really need, I really need time now, uh, yeah

So set me free
Freer than the open mind
Farther than the eyes can handle
Freer than the ocean now
Yeah, yeah

So, set me free
Now, I need to find release
Set me to the open sky
Now, I need to free my mind, yeah

I might be falling deep
I might be falling deep
I might be falling deep
I might be falling deep
Tell me now what you need
I've been going to God
When I'm all in my mind
I might be falling deep
Falling deep
I might be falling
I might be falling
I might be falling
I might be falling

Winter Whispers

"Wow, that's so inspiring," Paris said to herself, her voice tinged with wonder. "Yet, here I am, faced with winter in Georgia, where the cold whispers secrets and the streets echo with untold stories." She turned onto a deserted, bushy road leading to her off-grid smart office, hidden away from the bustling city.

The air was crisp, winter's approach making her breath visible with every exhale. Snow fell gently, blanketing the landscape in white. Paris paused for a moment, admiring the serene beauty. Reaching for her keys, the lock clicked open with a satisfying sound—a signal that her haven awaited.

After stepping out of her extraordinary Aston Martin, Paris took a deep breath, her resolve hardening. "After that message from Tems while driving this beauty, I feel unstoppable. I will get to the bottom of all this nonsense," she declared to herself.

Walking toward a hidden spot, she began pulling back bushes and twigs to reveal a concealed safe box. Inside lay the essentials for her mission: keys to her office, a small notebook, a plant-covered car cover, and three pre-rolled blue lotus flower blends designed to open her third eye. Paris gathered her items, feeling the weight of potential discoveries settle over her like a cloak.

The sun dipped below the horizon, casting an amber glow and stretching shadows along her path. Guided by intuition, she unlocked the door to her inconspicuous sanctuary. From the outside, it appeared to be an old, rusted trailer, but inside, it pulsed with vibrant energy—a perfect blend of cutting-edge technology and tranquil aesthetics.

Paris pressed a button, revealing a secret door that slid open to a spiral staircase. As she descended into a labyrinth of sleek machinery and glowing corridors, the rhythmic hum of computers mixed with the faint aroma of incense. Her senses sharpened, her purpose renewed.

Walls lined with digital displays flickered with real-time data streaming from around the globe. Paris moved swiftly through the chambers, her fingers gliding across touchscreens. Each command she issued refined the flood of information until layers of encryption gave way to secrets long buried.

"In time," she murmured, taking a slow draw from the blue lotus flower blend. The fragrant mist clouded her thoughts briefly, only to leave her mind sharper than before. Her focus returned as she vowed, "I will find all of you. Whatever's happening, it can't be hidden much longer."

Paris stepped away from the monitors and entered her meditation chamber, where soft music tuned to 432 Hz enveloped her in calming energy. Settling onto a cushion, she closed her eyes and let her mind wander through the intricate connections she'd uncovered. Flashes of clandestine meetings and hidden transactions flooded her thoughts, each one more vivid than the last. Piece by piece, she unraveled the threads, until one realization struck her like lightning.

"Miami!" she shouted, her eyes snapping open. In her vision, she saw a private jet carrying Miami toward an undisclosed location. "Fiddle sticks!" she muttered, frustrated by the loss of connection. Her white-gray eyes flickered to hazel as she returned to the present, refocusing her attention.

The digital map glowed before her, each point a potential lead. A new message appeared in her inbox from NovaGaia, encrypted with wisdom yet to be decoded. Paris hesitated for a moment, her fingers hovering over the keyboard. "Could this be the key?" she wondered aloud. Trusting her intuition, she decrypted the file.

Answers lie where shadows dance, it read, its prophetic words steeped in mystery. A memory surfaced—a small café in Montmartre, where shadows played tricks with the light. It had seemed insignificant at the time, but now it held new meaning. Paris knew this was her next step.

You know what Jams my Glock??
—Diamond

Chapter 6
THE INTERGALACTIC FEDERATION MEETS WITH MURDOCH

Meanwhile, Just'n Francois, deep in thought, sat in the back of his all-black SUV. "Miami …" he murmured, the name lingering in his mind. "I know I've seen that girl before." He could feel the puzzle pieces starting to fall into place.

The driver interrupted, "Where to, boss?"

"Check your device. The entire itinerary is there," Just'n replied, his tone distracted.
Suddenly, two mysterious men in all black entered the SUV. "Don't move," one of them demanded, pointing a Glock 17 at Just'n's head.

Just'n remained unbothered, pouring himself a glass of Goût de Diamants champagne. "Relax. Care for a glass? Fun fact, this is the most luxurious champagne in the world. A single cup costs €328,000," he said with a sly smile.

"Enough games," the Englishman barked. "We need you to report that CIA Agent Samantha has been found dead."

"Impossible. I can't report false news," Just'n retorted.

"You will," the Spaniard interjected. "Or face consequences." He slid a piece of paper toward Just'n. The number written on it was staggering—$300 million to fabricate the story.

Just'n sipped his champagne, his expression unreadable. "Generous, but not my line of work."

The tension in the SUV grew thick. Suddenly, the vehicle screeched to a halt. Outside, more men in black blocked the road. A chilling silence filled the air before chaos erupted. Gunfire rang out, blood splattered across Just'n's tailored suit, and his panic button—hidden under the champagne glass—was activated.

Within moments, Just'n's own security team arrived. "Are you okay, Mr. Francois?" one asked urgently.

Just'n wiped the blood from his face, calmly stepping out. "Fine. Now, get me a clean suit. I'm late for a press meeting," he said, kicking one of the attackers' bodies aside.

While his team cleaned up the scene, Just'n adjusted his tie, muttering, "Some people just don't understand business."

Just'n quickly reached for his iPhone 16 Pro Max, his hands trembling ever so slightly, and called his assistant.

"Yes, Mr. Francois," the assistant responded, her voice calm as she sipped her pine needle green tea deliberately, masking the chaos brewing in her mind.

"Heather," Just'n said, his voice low and clipped. "Handle it. I'm running late."

Inside the Board Room of WDCKI

Heather hesitated for a moment, knowing the implications. She immediately reached out to Just'n's colleagues, her fingers dancing across her phone screen like a pianist on their final encore.
"Mr. Francois will be delayed," she informed them, her voice steady but tight.

Deverist appeared on the video call, her image crisp against the backdrop of a Parisian skyline. The City of Light stretched behind her, the Eiffel Tower standing resolute amidst the fading hues of dusk. Yet, it was Deverist who commanded attention. Her skin, a rich, flawless brown, reflected the golden light streaming through her penthouse windows, giving her an almost ethereal glow. At 5'6" and 135 pounds, her model-like physique was a testament to both discipline and natural grace. Though she was forty, she could have easily passed for a woman half her age—a beauty that masked the sharp mind and ruthless instincts beneath.

"Late?" she repeated icily, her voice carrying a soft lilt that only heightened the tension. Her razor-sharp gaze swept over the faces of the board members on the other end of the call. She leaned slightly closer to the camera, her features perfectly framed by the soft glow of Parisian lights. "I don't tolerate 'late,' Heather. Not in my world."

Heather swallowed hard, keeping her composure while Deverist's presence seemed to fill the room despite being thousands of miles away. "I assure you, everything is under control, Mrs. Daugherty!" Heather replied carefully, her voice steady.

Deverist's expression didn't waver. Her beauty was a weapon, but her power lay in her ability to make others feel as though she knew their every secret, their every fear. She shifted slightly, the skyline behind her shimmering like a jewel-encrusted canvas. "Control is a fragile thing, Heather," she said, her tone laced with warning. "You'll find it slipping through your fingers if you hesitate for even a moment."

Miles away in Atlanta, the boardroom fell silent as the connection crackled slightly. Deverist's words carried weight, her influence a looming presence even from across an ocean. Just'n, usually unflinching, found himself drawn to her every word, her every movement on the screen. She was more than an ally—she was a force of nature.

"I'll handle this," Deverist declared, her tone leaving no room for argument. Her gaze flicked momentarily to the Eiffel Tower in the distance, its iron frame casting long shadows over the city. "I always handle it."

The video call ended abruptly, leaving the room in stunned silence. In her wake, Deverist left a charged atmosphere, a sense that whatever storm was brewing, she was both its architect and the only one capable of taming it.

Back in her Parisian penthouse, Deverist stepped away from the camera, her expression unreadable. The city's lights danced on the polished marble floors, but her mind was already racing ahead, calculating her next move. She knew this was no ordinary day. It wasn't just business—it was personal. Somewhere, hidden in the shadows of her empire, a thread was unraveling. And Deverist was determined to find it before it pulled everything apart.

Meanwhile, Back in Atlanta
Location: Peachtree Street, Buckhead

In the private boardroom of WDCKI, tension crackled like a live wire.

Just'n paced the room, his piercing gaze raking over the assembled board members. His words cut through the oppressive silence. "Who. Put. A hit on me?"

The question hung in the air like smoke, heavy and suffocating. No one dared to speak, but their unease was palpable. Finally, an older man at the far end of the table cleared his throat, his voice hesitant.

"It may not be a matter of *who*, but *why*, Mr. Francois. Perhaps someone sees you as a threat—or worse, this could be a warning."

Just'n's jaw tightened, his fingers drumming a sharp rhythm against the polished mahogany table. His mind churned, replaying recent events like fragments of a broken mirror.

"Such a bold move," he murmured, his voice low but dangerous, "means they're close. Too close."

"Close enough to know our next steps," the old man added gravely. "This wasn't random, Just'n. Someone's been watching—someone who knows more than they should."

Just'n's eyes narrowed, his voice cold and precise.
"Never mind who. I need to know *what* they want. And I want to know it *now*."

A woman with sharp eyes rose from her seat, her voice slicing through the tension.

"A preemptive strike is risky," she said, her tone both cautious and commanding. "But …" Her gaze met Just'n's. "It may be our only move."

"Exactly," Just'n replied, his lips curling into a grim smile. "We strike first—*and* we strike hard. But before that, we gather intel. Every detail, every lead."

His words were cut off by the sound of Siri chiming.

"You have an incoming message from Deverist," the AI announced.

"Read it," Just'n commanded.

Siri's robotic voice filled the room.

"This was an inside job—or an outsider who's had access to us for far too long without raising suspicion. End of message."
The room froze, the implications settling like a thundercloud.

The Shadows Grow Deeper

Samantha is alive.

The words hit Just'n like a sledgehammer, his breath catching as he stared out at the glittering Atlanta skyline. The city sprawled below him—a web of money, power, and deceit, laced with murder and betrayal.

"Isn't that what we always hoped—or feared?" someone murmured, their voice barely audible.

"That's absurd!" roared a burly Russian gentleman, slamming his palm onto the table. "She vanished without a trace *months* ago! We searched *everywhere*!"

"Not everywhere," Just'n said quietly, his voice laced with something dangerous. "If she's alive, it changes everything. And we *need* to know why she's resurfaced now."

"The media is circling," another voice interjected. "The leaks about the two girls? They've hit every major headline. It's chaos out there!"

"Exactly as planned," Just'n replied coldly. "The planted stories are doing their job—diverting attention from the real game. But we can't afford any mistakes. Every move must be calculated, every word rehearsed. If we slip ..." He trailed off, letting the unspoken consequences hang in the air.

He turned back to the group, his expression as sharp as the knife's edge.

"We're on a tightrope, and beneath us is the abyss. But if we play this right, we won't just survive. We'll *win*."

Silence stretched across the room. Outside, snow began to fall, blanketing the city in a deceptive stillness. But beneath the surface, the storm raged. And somewhere out there—in the shadows of the maze they'd built—the answers lay waiting.

Time was slipping through their fingers, and Just'n knew one thing for certain:

They were running out of it.

"I am a radiant vessel of divine love. Love flows to me, through me, and from me in perfect harmony with the universe. My heart and soul shine with infinite light."
—Paris D.

Chapter 7

THE AWAKENING

Zeke woke with a start, his chest heaving, the air in the cell heavy with the metallic tang of rain seeping through cracks in the walls. The storm outside roared, its fury shaking the prison. Lightning slashed across the sky, illuminating his sculpted face for a fleeting moment. Bronze skin glistened with sweat, his long, intricately twisted dreadlocks framing a jawline so sharp it could have been chiseled from stone. His dark eyes, piercing and filled with turmoil, scanned the room, searching for the remnants of the dream that had jolted him awake.

The visions were more than dreams. They were fragments of something he didn't yet understand but couldn't ignore. For weeks now, flashes of events he hadn't lived through—or hadn't yet—were invading his mind. They came without warning, like a flood breaching a dam, and left him shaken and breathless. He didn't know if it was a gift or a curse, but he knew one thing for certain: It was getting stronger.

Swinging his legs over the edge of the cot, Zeke planted his bare feet on the cold concrete floor. The rough texture bit into his skin, grounding him in the present moment. His towering physique, honed through years of discipline, moved with a fluid grace as he stood, every muscle tensed, every nerve on edge.

In the corner of the cell, hidden beneath a loose brick, lay his secret. Zeke knelt, the dim light casting sharp shadows across his chiseled features. His hands, calloused but steady, pried the brick loose. Beneath it, a scrap of paper and a small piece of charcoal waited. The paper was filled with frantic scrawls—names, dates, patterns he had deciphered from hushed conversations and stolen glances.

His eyes locked on a single name. Henderson. The man who had stolen everything from him. The man who had made him a prisoner, both in body and spirit.

"You think you've won," Zeke whispered, his voice low, rough, and filled with quiet fury.

A flicker of sensation—an electric hum just beneath his skin—ran through him. He clenched his fists, inhaling sharply. This strange force, this inexplicable awareness, was more vivid than ever. Closing his eyes, he saw flashes of the guard outside his cell, the jangle of keys, the faint scrape of boots on concrete. These weren't guesses. They weren't memories. They were certainties.

The storm outside swelled, a flash of lightning illuminating the defiance in his green eyes. He folded the paper carefully and tucked it into the waistband of his prison-issued pants. His long dreadlocks brushed his shoulders as he straightened, every movement deliberate, his body a coiled spring ready to strike.

Zeke's breath quickened, his heart hammering against his ribs. His newfound awareness frightened him, yet it sharpened his focus. Henderson had underestimated him. They all had.

His gaze flicked to the clock on the wall. The ticking seemed louder, the seconds stretching into eternity. Midnight approached, the storm outside raging in perfect rhythm with the storm inside him.

The guard's heavy boots echoed in the distance, growing closer with each step. Zeke stepped into the shadows, his bronze skin blending with the dim light. He ran a hand over his long dreadlocks, pushing them behind his shoulders. Every muscle in his body tensed, his sharp mind calculating the exact moment to move.

The visions struck again, stronger this time—flashes of chaos, a door swinging open, freedom inches away. They were no longer just hints of possibilities; they were a roadmap, leading him to the moment he'd been waiting for.

The storm roared, thunder shaking the walls. Zeke's dark eyes burned with determination, his jaw set. He was no longer just a man. He was a force, a predator, waiting for the perfect moment to strike.

Henderson thought he had broken him. He had no idea what he had unleashed.

As the clock struck midnight, the guard rounded the corner, keys jangling at his hip. Zeke's lips curved into a faint, dangerous smile.

The time for waiting was over.

It was time to act.

The storm outside roared louder, the wind screaming through the narrow prison windows. Zeke's heart hammered in his chest, but his mind sharpened with a clarity he hadn't felt in years. He pressed his back against the cold wall of his cell, his long bronze dreadlocks brushing his shoulders as he closed his eyes and willed himself to focus.

There it was again—the strange sensation he couldn't explain. It wasn't sight, not sound, but something deeper, something primal. Images and feelings flickered through his consciousness, disjointed and hazy yet unmistakable. The guard's pacing footsteps echoed in his mind before they even touched the ground. The rattle of keys was sharper, louder, as if it carried a hidden meaning only he could hear.

Zeke inhaled deeply, his breath steady despite the storm raging outside and within. He wasn't just imagining it. He could feel their intentions—hesitation, wariness, and just the faintest glimmer of fear. The pieces of his plan clicked together like a perfectly tuned symphony, and suddenly, he knew exactly when to move.

He opened his eyes. The faint flicker of fluorescent light above seemed to hum in rhythm with his heartbeat. This was his moment. Not just to escape, but to begin unraveling the mysteries tied to Henderson—and to himself.

The clock struck midnight, and a bolt of lightning illuminated the corridor. The guard turned the corner, his shadow stretching down the hall. Zeke straightened, every muscle poised, his mind sharper than a blade.

The storm's roar drowned out the first sound of footsteps. Then, silence.

Zeke whispered to himself, his voice low and resolute. "This ends tonight."

For the first time in years, Zeke wasn't just fighting to survive—he was ready to win.

Chapter 8
HENDERSON'S EMPIRE

Walter Henderson's office was more than an office—it was a monument to dominance. Towering bookshelves lined with first editions loomed over a sprawling mahogany desk while floor-to-ceiling windows framed the glittering city below, a kingdom he had carved from chaos. The air inside was heavy with the scent of aged leather and ambition, suffused with an unnatural quiet. Only the steady ticking of an antique clock dared to break the silence, marking the passage of time in a room where power seemed eternal.

Henderson sat at the center of it all, his sharp, angular features cast in the pale glow of flickering monitors. His tailored suit was immaculate, but there was a predatory tension in his posture. He exuded the controlled menace of a man who had risen from the ashes, shaped by fire, and forged into steel.

But tonight, despite the empire at his command, Walter Henderson felt a shadow in the air—something he hadn't felt in years.

A Memory of Fire

Henderson's gaze drifted toward the crackling fireplace, its flames a hypnotic dance that pulled him back to another fire, long ago. He was ten years old, lying on the frozen pavement outside his burning home, clutching his mother's wedding ring so tightly the band had cut into his palm. Smoke filled his lungs as the neighbors shouted, their faces blurred by tears and panic.

Inside, his father was screaming, drunk and trapped in a blaze of his own making. The fire consumed everything—his childhood, his innocence, and any illusions he had left about the world. Walter didn't cry. He watched the flames devour his father with the cold clarity of a boy who had learned his first brutal lessons:

1. The world doesn't care about fairness.
2. Only the ruthless survive.

By the time the embers cooled, Walter Henderson had already begun his transformation. The boy who escaped that fire had died alongside his father. In his place stood someone harder, sharper, and unrelenting.

The Cost of Power

Now, decades later, Walter Henderson had built an empire so vast, so unshakable, that even whispers of rebellion were crushed before they could take root. But power came at a price. Behind the polished façade, he battled his demons in solitude. Insomnia gripped him like a vice, each sleepless night haunted by the faces of those he'd crushed underfoot.

He kept a bottle of pills in the drawer of his desk, tucked beneath the pristine surface. He rarely used them. Weakness, even in private, was an indulgence he could not afford.

Still, tonight felt different. Zeke Cross's name had begun to echo in his mind, irritating him like a thorn he couldn't remove.

Henderson rose from his chair and strode to the window, the snowstorm outside blanketing the city in eerie silence. His reflection stared back at him—older, colder, but undeniably powerful. He clenched his jaw. Power wasn't given; it was taken, seized, and held with bloodstained hands.

He thought of Zeke.
A Protégé Turned Threat

Zeke had once been his protégé, the closest thing to family Henderson had allowed himself. The Brazilian's raw talent, ambition, and fire had reminded Walter of his younger self. Zeke's bronze dreadlocks, chiseled features, and magnetic charm had made him a star in Henderson's world, a rising power in the underworld.

But Zeke had one fatal flaw: ideals. His relentless belief in justice had made him fragile. Henderson had offered him the truth of the world—a seat at the table of power—but Zeke had rejected it. And in doing so, he had rejected Henderson.

"I gave you everything," Henderson murmured to the empty room, his voice low and venomous. "And you chose to betray me."

He tried to convince himself that Zeke's defiance was a nuisance, a loose thread to be cut away. But deep down, Henderson knew better. Zeke wasn't just another enemy. He was the one man who truly understood him. And that made him dangerous.

The Family He Left Behind

The thought of family tugged at the edges of Henderson's mind—a place he rarely allowed himself to go. His ex-wife, Clara, had walked away years ago, taking their son, Leo, with her.

"You don't want love, Walter," she had said on her way out. "You want control. And I won't let our son grow up in your shadow."

Her words had stung, though he'd never admit it. The custody battle for Leo had been the only battle he'd ever lost, and it had left a scar deeper than any wound he'd endured.

Now, Leo was a stranger, living a life Henderson couldn't touch. Sometimes, when he stared out over the city, he wondered if his son had inherited his fire—or his mother's quiet defiance.

But Walter shook the thought from his mind. Family was a distraction. Legacy, however, was eternal.

A Legacy in Flames

Walter turned back to his desk, his eyes narrowing on the monitors that displayed his empire in motion. Just'n and his ragtag team thought they could challenge him, thought they could topple a king.

"Fools," he muttered, his lips curling into a sneer. "Justice is a story the weak tell themselves to sleep at night. Power is the only truth."

Operation Eclipse wasn't just a plan; it was a declaration. Walter Henderson would not be brought low by idealists or dreamers. He would burn their hopes to ash.

And yet, the fire in his dreams lingered. Last night, he had dreamed of the flames again, the smoke thick in his lungs, the heat searing his skin. But this time, when he had looked into the inferno, it wasn't his father he saw.

It was Zeke.

The Shadow of Doubt

The intercom buzzed, breaking the silence.

"Mercer," Henderson barked, his voice sharp.

"Yes, sir?"

"I want every resource we have on Zeke Cross. Every move he makes, every word he speaks—I want it reported directly to me."

"Yes, sir."

Henderson sat back in his chair, steeping his fingers as he stared into the monitors.

"Let's see what you're really made of, Zeke," he murmured, his voice low and dangerous. "Because if you fail, I'll burn your world to the ground."

Outside, the storm raged on, but inside, Henderson felt a deeper storm brewing—one that threatened to consume everything he had built.

This wasn't just about power anymore. It was personal.

"I am aligned with the highest frequency of love. Love fills every cell of my being, radiating peace, joy, and harmony into the world around me."
—Paris D.

Chapter 9

CROSSHAIRS

The drive back to headquarters was cloaked in an uneasy stillness, the snow falling in relentless waves that painted Georgia in a ghostly white. Inside the car, Agent Dixon's jaw was tight, his knuckles white as they gripped the steering wheel. The rhythmic crunch of snow beneath the tires was the only sound, but his mind was anything but quiet.

Two days ago, he had kissed Paris goodbye at their modest house on the edge of the city. She had stood barefoot in their kitchen, bathed in the soft morning light, her wild blonde curls tumbling over her shoulders, wearing nothing but one of his faded shirts. She had smiled faintly, but the light behind her blue eyes hadn't reached him—not fully.

"Be safe," she had murmured, her voice as soft as the snow falling now.

He had kissed her forehead, promising he would. But now, as the cold outside seeped through the windows, a darker thought clawed at him: *Had she been wishing him safety or buying herself time?*

A Life Built on Lies

Dixon pulled into the driveway of the safe house and killed the engine. He sat there, staring through the windshield as the snowflakes clung to the glass, refusing to melt. His breath fogged the air as he exhaled, but the chill in his chest wasn't from the cold.

For months, he had tried to silence the doubts, to ignore the unanswered questions that gnawed at the foundation of his relationship with Paris. She had never hidden her past—her years as a hitwoman, the lies she had told to infiltrate his life under the guise of an assistant. He had forgiven her, convinced himself that love could survive even the sharpest betrayal.

But lately, something in her had shifted. She was quieter, her laughter muted, her movements careful. And then there was her connection to Miami—the ghostly assassin who had eluded every agency, every trap, for years. Miami wasn't just a professional target; she was personal. Paris's friend. Paris's past.

Dixon climbed out of the car, the snow crunching under his boots as he approached the door. He tried to shake the thought that had been haunting him since the mission began: If Miami is near Paris, then Paris is still in the game.

And if that was true, then everything between them might be a lie.

The Shot That Changed Everything

The safe house was dimly lit, the faint hum of a space heater was the only sound as Dixon tossed his bag onto the worn couch. The smell of old wood and dust filled the air, dragging him back to a different time, a different place.

Atlanta. Three months ago.

The warehouse had been a labyrinth of shadows and rusted metal, the air thick with mildew and tension. Dixon had moved silently through the darkness, Samantha Wright at his side. She had been his partner for three years—sharp, unyielding, and fiercely loyal. At least, that's what he'd believed.

The memory played out like a nightmare in his mind.

The mission had gone sideways in an instant—gunfire erupted, chaos swallowed the room, and in the middle of it all, Samantha turned to him. Her gun was raised, her eyes wide, her face a mix of desperation and something else: regret.

The shot came before he could process it, the burning pain ripping through his side as he fell. The betrayal was worse than the bullet.

And then she was hit. Blood pooled beneath her as she crumpled to the ground. He had thought she was dead.

But now, staring at the photo he had found earlier, her face staring back at him, he knew better. Samantha was alive. And if she was alive, everything he thought he knew about that night was wrong.

Operation Mongoose

Dixon dropped the photo onto the table, his fingers brushing the edges of the paper as if it might dissolve under his touch. Operation Mongoose wasn't just another mission—it was a war against a network of assassins, arms dealers, and the corrupt forces that protected them.

And at the center of it all was Miami.

She was the lynchpin, the ghost who tied it all together. But tracking her wasn't just about strategy; it was about Paris. If Miami was back, then so was Paris's connection to her—a connection that could destroy everything.

He poured himself a glass of rum from the bottle he kept in the cabinet, the rich scent filling the room as he took a slow sip. The warmth spread through him, but it did nothing to ease the tension in his chest.

He thought of his grandmother's words, spoken years ago on their porch in Kingston, while the sunset painted the sky in fiery hues.

"Power doesn't come free, child," she had said, her voice heavy with wisdom and warning. "Yuh haffi choose. Choose how much yuh willin' to lose."

Dixon had thought he understood then. But now, as he stared at the tangled mess of his life, he wasn't so sure.

The Call

His phone buzzed, the sound cutting through the silence.

"Dixon," he said, his voice sharp.

"We have a lead," Harding said on the other end.

Dixon's pulse quickened. "What kind of lead?"

"It's Paris. Surveillance caught her leaving the house earlier. She parked her car and went on foot into the woods."

The words hit him like a punch. "Why the hell would she—"

"Don't know yet," Harding interrupted. "We're working on it. Danvers is analyzing the footage now."

Dixon clenched his jaw. "Send me what you've got."

Moments later, the file came through. He opened it, his breath hitching as the grainy footage played on his screen. Paris exited her car, her movements hurried but deliberate. She glanced around, her expression unreadable, before disappearing into the woods.

The camera panned to the edge of the trail. Behind a cluster of bushes with vibrant flowers blooming despite the snow, something glinted in the dim light.

"What is she doing?" Dixon muttered.

"We're not sure yet," Harding replied. "But we'll find out."

The call ended, leaving Dixon alone with the footage.

A Choice to Make

He replayed the video, analyzing every movement, every detail. Was she hiding something? Meeting someone? Or was she just running?

Dixon's chest tightened as he realized the choice before him. Confront the woman he loved and risk losing her—or use her as bait to find Miami and end this mission once and for all.

He stared at the screen, the faint echo of his grandmother's voice lingering in his mind: ***"Choose how much yuh willing to lose."***

"I am a magnet for abundance. Wealth flows to me effortlessly and in divine alignment with my highest good. I attract prosperity in all forms, and my financial blessings are limitless."
—Paris D.

Chapter 10

BREAKING THE CHAINS

The prison was a fortress of steel and stone, a place designed not just to hold people but to break them. Every surface was cold and unyielding, every corner watched by hidden cameras and motion sensors. Even the air felt oppressive, tinged with a faint metallic smell, like blood and rust.

Zeke had been in his share of bad places, but nothing like this. The walls seemed to hum with power, charged by the massive generators that kept the facility operational. Every door was reinforced with bulletproof alloy, and the faint blue glow of energy fields crackled around high-priority areas.

The prison's corridors were a maze, deliberately designed to confuse and disorient. Without Just'n's map and Yasmeen's sharp instincts, Zeke knew he'd be lost in minutes. Yet, even as he followed their lead, that strange energy inside him kept pulling at his attention like it was alive.

The Security Systems

They passed a series of wall-mounted security panels, their screens glowing faintly in the dim light. Zeke caught glimpses of guards on patrol, prisoners pacing in their cells, and even drone-like machines hovering through maintenance shafts.

"Stay close," Just'n whispered, his hazel eyes scanning the hallway ahead. "If one of those drones spots us, we're done."

Zeke nodded but couldn't help glancing back at the nearest panel. He felt a strange pull, like he could almost reach out and touch it—even from several feet away.

"Focus," Yasmeen hissed, her green eyes narrowing as she glanced back at him. "We're not here to admire the tech."

The Tension Mounts

The team moved quickly but cautiously, their footsteps muffled by the specially designed rubber soles of their boots. The corridors were eerily quiet, save for the distant hum of the generators and the faint buzz of fluorescent lights.

Ahead, the faint glow of a checkpoint came into view. Two guards stood in front of a sealed door, its surface reinforced with layers of what looked like titanium and graphene plating. A retinal scanner blinked to life as one of the guards shifted, scanning his eye with a faint beep.

Zeke felt his stomach tighten. This wasn't just a prison—it was a war machine.

"East corridor," Zeke whispered, his voice barely audible. "Three guards. One has a radio, but it's off for now."

Yasmeen turned, her sharp gaze locking onto his. "How—"

"Trust me," Zeke interrupted, his tone more forceful than he intended.

A Deadly Encounter

The team took a detour to avoid the checkpoint, slipping into a side corridor marked with hazard signs. The walls here were lined with pipes and conduits, many of them sparking faintly. Steam hissed from broken valves, and the air was thicker, warmer.

Ahead, Yasmeen slowed, her movements catlike as she signaled for them to stop. She crouched low, her green eyes scanning the dimly lit hall ahead.

Two guards stood at the next intersection, their weapons slung casually across their chests. They were chatting quietly, their voices blending with the hum of the machinery around them.

Yasmeen's blade was in her hand before Zeke even registered her movement. She advanced silently, her footsteps impossibly light.

The first guard didn't even have time to scream. Yasmeen was on him in a flash, her blade slicing cleanly through his throat. She caught his body as it fell, lowering it gently to the ground.

The second guard turned, his eyes widening in shock. Just'n stepped in, grabbing him by the neck and slamming him against the wall with a sickening crack.

"Clean," Yasmeen whispered, wiping her blade on the dead guard's uniform.

A Fateful Connection

As they moved deeper into the facility, Zeke couldn't shake the feeling of being watched. It wasn't just the cameras—he felt the prison itself, as if the walls were alive, pulsing with energy.

"Wait," he said, stopping abruptly.

"What now?" Yasmeen snapped, her patience wearing thin.

Zeke turned to the nearest security panel, his hazel-green eyes narrowing. The faint glow of the screen seemed to call to him. Without thinking, he reached out, his fingers brushing the smooth surface.

The screen flickered. Lines of code appeared, scrolling too quickly for anyone else to read.

"What are you doing?" Yasmeen demanded, grabbing his arm.

Zeke pulled back, shaking his head. "I don't know. It just … happened."

Just'n glanced between them, his expression unreadable. "We don't have time for this. Move."

The Control Room

They reached a control room—an unoccupied nerve center filled with monitors and consoles. Zeke hesitated, his chest tightening as he stepped inside.

The screens displayed live feeds from every corner of the prison: guards patrolling, prisoners locked in their cells, and high-tech drones scanning the facility. One feed showed the extraction point—a service tunnel leading to the outside.

"Malik and Raquel are pinned down," Just'n said, his voice grim. "We need to get there now."

Zeke's eyes darted to another screen, his heart pounding. He saw something the others didn't—a group of guards moving toward the service tunnel from an adjacent corridor.

"It's a trap," Zeke said, his voice barely above a whisper.

Just'n turned to him sharply. "How do you know that?"

Zeke met his gaze, his voice steady. "Because I can see it."

For a moment, no one spoke. Then, Just'n nodded. "Secondary exit. Two levels down. Let's go."

The Descent

The air grew colder as they descended into the lower levels. The walls here were rougher, the lighting dimmer. Water dripped from unseen pipes, the sound echoing in the narrow stairwell.

"This place feels like a tomb," Yasmeen muttered, her green eyes darting around.

"Stay focused," Just'n said, his tone sharp.

Zeke led the way, his instincts guiding him through the labyrinth of tunnels. He could feel the energy inside him growing stronger, pulling him toward the exit like an invisible thread.

Finally, they reached the secondary exit—a rusted storm drain that led outside. Malik and Raquel were waiting, their faces pale and bloodied but alive.

Unanswered Questions

As they regrouped near the extraction vehicle, Yasmeen cornered Zeke.

"You knew about the trap, the guards, even the layout of this place," she said, her voice low but fierce. "What aren't you telling us?"

Zeke hesitated, his hazel-green eyes flickering with uncertainty. "I don't know how to explain it. I just … feel things."

Yasmeen studied him, her expression hard. "You're not normal, Zeke. And whatever this is—it's dangerous."

Before he could respond, Just'n called out. "We're moving! Now!"

The team climbed into the vehicle, the engine roaring as they sped into the snowy night.

Zeke sat in silence, the weight of Yasmeen's words pressing on him. She was right—he wasn't normal. The energy inside him wasn't just growing—it was evolving.

And deep down, he feared it might destroy them all.

The Frosted Night

The storm drain's exit led to a barren, frost-covered landscape. Snow blanketed the ground, the pale moonlight illuminating the team's hurried escape. The extraction vehicle rumbled beneath them, its tires kicking up icy slush as it sped away from the fortress behind them.

Inside the vehicle, the silence was deafening, broken only by the hum of the engine and the occasional crackle of the team's comms.

Malik, cradling his rifle, glanced at Zeke. "You're full of surprises, man."

Zeke didn't answer. His hands were clenched tightly in his lap, his gaze fixed out the window.

Yasmeen sat across from him, her piercing green eyes never leaving his face. She didn't trust him—not fully. Not yet. And Zeke couldn't blame her.

The Burning Truth

As the vehicle rumbled on, Zeke felt the energy inside him again. It wasn't as chaotic as before; now, it simmered, steady and relentless. It was like a second heartbeat, one that didn't belong to him but refused to let him go.

He closed his eyes, willing himself to relax, but the visions returned. Flashes of faces he didn't recognize, places he'd never been, and something else—a shape cloaked in shadow, watching from the depths of his mind.

Yasmeen's voice snapped him back to reality.

"You've got answers, Zeke," she said, her tone sharp. "And you're going to share them. Maybe not now, but soon."

Zeke met her gaze, the glow in his hazel-green eyes faint but undeniable. "If I had answers, Yasmeen, I'd give them to you."

She studied him for a long moment before leaning back, her expression unreadable.

The Weight of the Unknown

Just'n, sitting in the front, turned slightly. "We've got a safe house about twenty miles out. We'll regroup there and figure out our next move."

The team murmured their agreement, but the weight of their escape hung heavy in the air. They'd made it out, but barely. And whatever was happening with Zeke had just raised the stakes for all of them.

The Closing Thought

Zeke leaned his head back against the cold metal wall of the vehicle. The snow outside fell harder now, the flakes swirling like ghosts in the wind.

For the first time, he felt more than fear. He felt purpose—a deep, unshakable certainty that whatever was happening to him wasn't a coincidence. It was part of something bigger.

But that certainty came with a cost.

Because with every vision, every pulse of energy, Zeke felt something else creeping into his mind.

It wasn't just power. It was something darker.

And he wasn't sure how long he could hold it back.

Chapter 11

BONDS FORGED IN SHADOWS

The safe house wasn't a dingy hideout in some forgotten corner of the city. It was a penthouse suite perched high above the glittering skyline of downtown Chicago. Floor-to-ceiling windows framed the view, showcasing snow-dusted skyscrapers and the icy expanse of Lake Michigan in the distance. The space was sleek and modern, with marble floors, plush leather furnishings, and a grand chandelier casting a soft golden glow over the room.

Zeke stood near the window, a glass of top-shelf whiskey in his hand. His bronze dreadlocks framed his face, and the dim light caught the striking mix of hazel and green in his eyes. He wore tailored black pants and a crisp white shirt—a far cry from the itchy prison uniform he had endured for far too long.

"Still doesn't feel real," he muttered, his gaze fixed on the city below.

Yasmeen reclined on the sprawling sectional sofa, her radiant green eyes watching him with quiet intensity. Her long black hair spilled over her shoulders, and her fitted silk dress accentuated her model-like frame. She held a crystal glass of wine, swirling the deep red liquid idly as she studied Zeke.

"It's real," she said, her Russian accent soft but unmistakable. "You're free. That's what matters."

Just'n emerged from the open-concept kitchen, a plate of charcuterie in one hand and his own glass of whiskey in the other. He wore a sleek, custom-tailored suit that seemed to radiate confidence and power. At 6'3", his presence dominated the room, and the warmth of his hazel eyes belied the sharp mind always at work behind them.

"You'll get used to it," Just'n said, setting the plate on the coffee table. "This life. The freedom. The luxury. You've earned it, Zeke."

Zeke turned from the window, his expression skeptical. "Earned it? You two are out here living like royalty, and I was rotting in a cell."

Yasmeen tilted her head, a faint smile playing on her lips. "We all have our roles, Zeke. Yours just took … a different path."

A Shared History

The room fell into a brief silence, the faint sound of jazz playing from the hidden speakers filling the space. Yasmeen leaned forward, her green eyes locking onto Zeke's.

"Do you remember Moscow?" she asked, her tone light but her gaze unrelenting.

Zeke let out a low laugh, shaking his head. "How could I forget? That alleyway was freezing. And you … You showed up like some kind of assassin angel."

Yasmeen smirked, taking a sip of her wine. "And you were about to die. I saved you."

"Barely," Zeke shot back, his grin widening. "I think I did most of the work."

Just'n chuckled, taking a seat across from them. "This sounds familiar.

Yasmeen saving someone while pretending she didn't care?"

Yasmeen arched an elegant brow. "Careful, Just'n. Shall we talk about Istanbul? Or do you want to keep pretending you didn't almost blow your cover?"

Just'n held up his hands in mock surrender. "Hey, I got us out, didn't I?"

"Barely," Yasmeen retorted, her voice dripping with playful sarcasm.

Zeke's Reflection

Zeke watched the two of them banter, a warm feeling settling in his chest despite himself. He had always felt like the odd one out in their trio. Yasmeen and Just'n were larger than life—wealthy, powerful, and always in control. Meanwhile, he had spent most of his life scraping by, trying to survive in a world that seemed determined to crush him.

But as he looked at them now, laughing and relaxed, he realized something.

They weren't just allies. They were family.

"Hey," he said, his voice cutting through the laughter.

Yasmeen and Just'n turned to him, their expressions softening.

"Thank you," Zeke said simply. "For everything. For not giving up on me."

Just'n leaned back, his hazel eyes thoughtful. "We don't leave our own behind, Zeke. Not ever."

Yasmeen raised her glass, her green eyes sparkling. "To freedom," she said, her voice carrying a hint of emotion.

Zeke and Just'n raised their glasses in return, the clink of crystal ringing through the room.

The Question

As the night wore on, the three of them settled into a comfortable silence. The city lights twinkled outside, a reminder of the world waiting for them beyond the safety of the penthouse.

Zeke's thoughts drifted to the visions he had experienced during the escape—the unexplainable flashes that had guided them to safety. He glanced at Yasmeen, wondering if she had noticed something.

She met his gaze, her green eyes unreadable. For a moment, he thought she might say something, but she only offered a small, knowing smile.

Just'n broke the silence. "What's next?"

Yasmeen set her glass down, her expression turning serious. "We need to focus on Henderson. He's not going to stop. And now that we've broken Zeke out, he'll be coming for us."

Zeke nodded, his jaw tightening. "Then we hit him first."

The resolve in his voice was unmistakable, and for the first time, Yasmeen saw a glimpse of the man Zeke was becoming—a leader, not just a survivor.

"We will," she said, her voice steady. "But we need a plan. And we need to find Autumn before it's too late."

Just'n stood, his commanding presence filling the room. "Then we start tomorrow. For now, get some rest. It's going to be a long fight."

While Zeke watched him walk away, he felt a surge of determination. He wasn't just fighting for himself anymore. He was fighting for the people who had risked everything to save him.

And he wasn't going to let them down.

The room fell into a contemplative silence, each person lost in their own thoughts.

"I am limitless. I rise above all challenges with strength, wisdom, and confidence. The universe supports my every step, and success is my destiny."
—Paris D.

Chapter 12

THE OCEAN'S ADVOCATE

Amy Lyons stepped out into the brisk Atlanta morning, the world around her humming with life. The air was sharp, tinged with the metallic scent of impending snow. Overhead, a flock of sparrows darted across the pale sky, their chirping cutting through the quiet like notes from an unseen symphony.

She paused on the sidewalk, closing her eyes to feel the subtle shifts around her. The trees lining the street whispered in the wind, their bare branches rattling softly. Somewhere in the distance, a squirrel scurried across the frosted ground, the sound faint but distinct to Amy's finely tuned senses.

The environment was her sanctuary, her compass. She could feel the city holding its breath, as though the earth itself was wary of the chaos lurking beneath its surface.

The Warehouse Investigation

The remnants of the warehouse loomed ahead, the scene stark against the backdrop of the gray sky. Snowflakes began to fall, light and unassuming, melting as soon as they touched the charred debris. Amy crouched near the ruins, her gloved hand brushing over the scorched earth.

The ground was cold, almost unnaturally so, as if it still held the memory of the violence that had occurred here. Amy shivered, not from the temperature but from the energy that lingered in the air.

She tilted her head, listening. The usual city sounds—car engines, distant chatter—were muffled here. Instead, she heard the faintest rustle of leaves from a nearby tree, a lone crow cawing as it circled overhead. Nature seemed uneasy, its balance disrupted by the brutality of human actions.

Amy's fingers found a fragment of one of the goat masks, its edges blackened and brittle. She held it up to the light, her green eyes narrowing. The material felt wrong—unnatural, almost out of place in this setting. She tucked it into a sample bag, her mind already racing with possibilities.

The Gift of Awareness

As she rose, Amy turned her face to the sky, letting the snowflakes melt on her skin. She could feel the atmosphere shifting, the wind carrying whispers of change. It was a sensation she had known since childhood, a connection to the earth that defied explanation.

Her parents had once called it a blessing, though her father often joked it was simply "the Irish knack for noticing everything." But Amy knew it was more than that. She could sense when the tides were off, when the birds flew in patterns they shouldn't, when the trees groaned under the weight of unseen burdens.

And now, as she stood in the aftermath of the warehouse explosion, she felt that same unease. The air here was thick, heavy with something she couldn't name. It was as though the land itself was crying out, urging her to uncover the truth.

Connecting the Dots

Back in her eco-friendly office, Amy spread out the maps and satellite images she had been studying. Her cat, Darwin, leapt onto the desk, purring softly as he nuzzled her arm. Amy absentmindedly stroked his fur, her eyes scanning the overlays of crime scenes and oceanic data.

She could see the pattern forming, like a constellation waiting to be connected. Atlanta, Seattle, and the Arctic Circle—each location tied not just to the goat masks but to the planet itself. The materials used, the preservation methods—they spoke of someone who understood the natural world as deeply as she did, but who used that knowledge for destruction.

Amy's thoughts drifted to her upcoming trip to the Galápagos Islands. The reports of illegal fishing and coral bleaching there weighed heavily on her heart. She felt torn between her duty as a detective and her calling as a marine biologist. But perhaps the two weren't so different. Both were about protecting life, about seeking justice for those who couldn't speak for themselves.

A New Lead

The snowfall outside intensified, blanketing the city in white. Amy watched from her window while the trees swayed gently, their branches etched against the sky like black veins. The sound of the snow was soothing, a quiet rhythm that reminded her of waves lapping against the shore.

Her phone buzzed, pulling her from her thoughts.

"Lyons," she answered.

"We've got something new," the voice on the other end said. "Another mask, found in Seattle. It's intact, and we're sending it to your lab now."

Amy's pulse quickened. The pattern was growing clearer. The coastal cities, the marine connections—it all pointed to something larger, something global.

She hung up, her green eyes flickering with determination. The world was out of balance, and she could feel it in her bones. The warehouse case wasn't just about human violence—it was about humanity's relationship with the planet itself.

Later that night, Amy stood on her balcony, the city quiet beneath the thick snow. She closed her eyes, inhaling the crisp air, letting it fill her lungs. She could feel the world's pulse, its rhythm slower than usual, as though it, too, was trying to heal.

The goat masks, the violence—they were symptoms of a deeper sickness. But Amy had spent her life fighting for the planet, for its oceans and its creatures. And now, she would fight for the truth.

As the snow fell around her, she made a silent promise to the earth she loved: She wouldn't stop until the balance was restored.

Amy had just settled into her desk chair, Darwin curled up beside her, when her phone vibrated against the wood. She glanced at the caller ID and smiled faintly.

"Hi, Da," she answered, tucking the phone between her ear and shoulder while she continued typing.

Her father's voice boomed through the line, his thick Irish accent unmistakable. "Amy, I've been watching the news. Another explosion, aye? And you're right in the middle of it again, aren't you?"

"Not in the middle," she assured him. "I'm investigating from a safe distance."

Her father snorted. "Safe distance, my foot. You've got red hair and your mother's stubborn streak—trouble's drawn to you like moths to a flame."

Amy chuckled softly. "I'll take that as a compliment."

"It's not," he replied gruffly. Then, after a pause, his tone softened. "You're careful, though, aren't you? You've got a good head on your shoulders, but I worry, lass. Your work takes you to dark places."

"I know, Da. But someone has to go there. Someone has to make sense of it all."

"Aye," he muttered. "But don't forget where you came from. There's always a place for you here, you know that. The lake's as beautiful as ever, and your mother's been baking those scones you like."

Amy's heart ached at the thought of Lake Erne, its dark, mysterious waters a sharp contrast to the chaos of Atlanta. "I miss it," she admitted.

"Then come home for a visit," he urged. "Just for a while. The world can wait a bit longer, can't it?"

Amy smiled wistfully. "Maybe soon. Thanks, Da."

A Mother's Concern

An hour later, her phone buzzed again, this time with her mother's name on the screen. Amy sighed, knowing exactly where this conversation was headed.

"Hi, Mum," she greeted, trying to sound cheerful.

"Amy, love," her mother said, her voice warm but laced with worry. "How are you eating? Proper meals, I hope—not just those rabbit food salads of yours."

"They're not rabbit food, Mum," Amy said with a laugh. "And yes, I'm eating fine."

"Good, because you've got that pale look about you lately. Have you been getting enough sun? And don't forget to take your vitamins."

"I'm fine, really," Amy insisted, though she knew her mother wouldn't let it go so easily.

"And what about that explosion I read about?" her mother continued. "Are you sure you're safe? This case of yours sounds awfully dangerous."

"It's no more dangerous than usual," Amy said gently. "I promise I'm being careful."

Her mother sighed. "We just worry, that's all. Your da and I, we sit by the lake and wonder if you've taken on too much. You've always been so determined, even as a little girl. But don't forget to take care of yourself, too."

Amy felt a pang of guilt. She hadn't visited her parents in years, her work and travels keeping her too busy. "I'll come home soon," she promised. "I miss you both—and the lake."

Her mother's voice softened. "It's beautiful this time of year. The mist rolls in every morning, and it's like something out of a fairytale. It'd do you good to see it again."

"I'll make time," Amy said, meaning it.

A Reminder of Home

After hanging up, Amy stared out the window, the snow falling steadily now. She thought of Lake Erne, its deep, mysterious waters and the stories her father used to tell her about the creatures that lived beneath its surface. It was a place of wonder and quiet magic, it was something that kept her mind off the chaos she faced in her workplace .

Her parents' calls always left her feeling torn between the life she'd chosen and the simpler one she'd left behind. But she knew she couldn't stop now. There were answers to find, justice to deliver.

Darwin stretched lazily on the desk, and Amy reached out to scratch behind his ears. "Soon, Darwin," she murmured. "We'll visit them soon."

But for now, her focus remained on the case. The goat masks, the Arctic traces, the uneasy feeling in the air—it was all connected. And Amy was determined to find the thread that would unravel it all.

"I am destined for greatness. Success flows to me effortlessly as I
align with my purpose, take inspired action, and trust in my limitless
potential."
—Paris D.

Chapter 13
TIDES OF TRUTH

The day Amy Lyons agreed to the Seattle mission it had begun with the shrill sound of her encrypted phone vibrating against the bamboo desk in her home office. She was elbow-deep in a proposal to increase protections for Georgia's coastal waters when the call came through. The caller ID was a secure line—a code she recognized instantly.

She wiped her hands on her eco-friendly sweater and picked up.

"This is Lyons."

The voice on the other end was firm but clipped. "We've got a situation in Seattle. Local authorities found a goat mask, similar to the ones from your Atlanta warehouse case, near a series of dead marine life washed ashore."

Amy's pulse quickened. "And you think they're connected?"

"Possibly. But that's not the disturbing part. The mask shows traces of North Pacific algae—and microplastics. We need someone who can connect the dots. Someone with your … expertise."

"I'm already stretched thin," Amy protested, glancing at the mounting pile of work on her desk. Meetings with oceanographers, advocacy groups, and her forensics team were scheduled for the week. But her mind was already racing.

The voice didn't waver. "This isn't optional. If this is part of Henderson's network, we can't afford to lose momentum. And you're the best we've got."

Amy closed her eyes, exhaling deeply. "Fine. But I'll need full access to any evidence—and control of the scene."

"Done. A flight's been arranged. Wheels up in three hours."

The Flight to Seattle

Amy moved quickly, canceling three meetings and delegating tasks to her junior detectives. She packed light, fitting everything into a sleek, carbon-neutral carry-on. Among her clothes and toiletries were the essentials of her trade: a custom laptop with forensic software, a portable spectrometer, and her multi-functional eco-gadget—a smartwatch capable of scanning soil, air, and water for chemical anomalies.

Before leaving, she slipped a GPS tracker into Darwin's collar and refilled his automated feeder. The cat meowed plaintively as she knelt to scratch his ears. "Don't worry, Darwin. I won't be gone long."

The cab ride to the airport was a blur, her thoughts consumed by the case. Who was behind the masks? Why the connection to the oceans? And what role, if any, did Henderson play?

Once on the plane, Amy ignored the in-flight entertainment and pulled up the case file on her tablet. Her fingers flew across the screen as she cross-referenced marine ecosystems, criminal networks, and the goat head mask murders. The more she read, the clearer it became that this wasn't just a regional issue. This was global.

The Arrival in Seattle

The descent into Seattle brought a jarring mix of turbulence and breathtaking views. The clouds parted just enough to reveal the jagged peaks of the Cascades and the endless expanse of Puget Sound. Amy's heart twisted at the sight of the ocean, so close yet so elusive.

By the time she stepped off the plane, her mind was in full mission mode. She declined the waiting car and instead rented an eco-friendly electric vehicle, her go-bag slung over her shoulder. The field office was less than an hour away, but Amy took a detour, stopping at the shoreline to collect a water sample.

She crouched by the edge, the cold wind biting her cheeks. Her smartwatch buzzed as it analyzed the sample. Elevated levels of pollutants—plastics, heavy metals, and traces of something she couldn't yet identify. Her brows knitted. Whatever was happening, it was bigger than she'd thought.

Field Office Briefing

The Seattle field office was a sterile, gray building tucked into a quiet industrial district. Amy was met by a local agent, a no-nonsense woman named Rivera, who handed her a report and led her to the evidence room.

"This is what we've got so far," Rivera said, pointing to the goat mask under a glass case. "Goat skin, same as Atlanta. But the fibers contain microplastics and algae native to the Pacific. We also found strands of fishing net woven into the edges."

Amy examined the mask closely, her gloved fingers brushing the coarse material. "And the bodies?"

Rivera hesitated. "Four dolphins, washed ashore near Bainbridge Island. Their stomachs were full of plastic, but the cause of death was blunt force trauma. Like they'd been … beaten."

Amy's stomach churned. She thought of Henderson's network; his nephew, Diego's, violent tendencies; and the warehouse explosion. It all felt connected, but the how and why eluded her.

Amy's Gadgets in Action

Amy set up a temporary workspace in the lab, unpacking her tools with precision. She connected her spectrometer to the mask, scanning for chemical markers. The results came back in seconds: traces of industrial waste and synthetic fibers commonly used in deep-sea fishing.

She moved to her laptop, pulling up satellite data to map ocean currents near Bainbridge Island. The patterns suggested something deliberate—like the bodies and the mask had been dumped at sea, carried by the tides to their discovery point.

Her smartwatch beeped, signaling an anomaly in the water sample she'd taken earlier. She plugged it into her laptop, her heart sinking as the data loaded. The unidentified substance was a synthetic compound used in illegal deep-sea drilling operations.

Amy leaned back in her chair, the pieces starting to fall into place. Someone was exploiting the ocean—polluting it, desecrating its creatures, and leaving a trail of violence in their wake.

That night, Amy sat alone in her hotel room, the rain tapping against the window. She stared at the city lights reflected in the dark waters of Puget Sound.

Her phone buzzed. A message from her mother: *Don't work too hard, love. And don't forget to call your da.*
Amy smiled faintly but didn't reply. She couldn't. Not yet.

The ocean called to her, its whispers growing louder with every clue she uncovered. The case wasn't just about the warehouse or the masks anymore. It was about something far more profound—and far more dangerous.

She would find the answers. She had to. For the oceans, for the creatures that depended on them, and for the planet itself.

Overworked!

Amy had barely begun analyzing her findings from the Seattle shoreline when her encrypted phone buzzed again. She rubbed her temples, exhaustion from the relentless case already settling in, and swiped to answer.

"Lyons," she said, her voice clipped but professional.

It was Tasha Bellamy, one of the lead agents from her Atlanta forensics team, calling from the east coast. The urgency in her tone was palpable.

"Amy, we need you in Portland. Immediately."

Amy frowned. "Portland? Tasha, I've just started breaking down the Seattle evidence. I can't drop this now."

"You'll want to," Tasha pressed. "They've found another goat head mask, but this one … Amy, it's tied directly to the marine events."

Amy straightened in her chair, heart pounding. "How?"

"Field agents uncovered it inside a fishing trawler at the Port of Portland. The ship's manifest is falsified, but its origin point traces back to the Pacific garbage gyre," Tasha explained. "There's more. The trawler's cargo included large barrels of waste—synthetic oils, microplastics, and a substance our lab is still working to identify. But here's the kicker: There were human remains in the waste. Skeletal fragments."

Amy's stomach tightened, but Tasha wasn't finished.

"They also found an engraving on the hull of the ship: a trident. The same symbol from the Seattle lead."

Amy leaned forward, her pen scratching rapidly across her notepad. "Are there any ties to Henderson or Diego?"

"We're working on it. But we're starting to think this isn't just about Henderson's operation anymore. This could be part of a larger network," Tasha said, lowering her voice. "Amy, this might be global."

Amy glanced at the evidence she'd spread out on her makeshift desk. The Seattle case was still raw, full of unanswered questions, but the gravity of Tasha's call left little room for doubt.

"I'll head to Portland," Amy said finally. "Keep me updated on the lab analysis, and send everything you have on that trawler to my secure account."

The Flight to Portland

Amy's departure from Seattle was a blur of packing, coordination, and logistics. Her eco-friendly rental was returned, and she caught a last-minute flight to Portland, using the hours in transit to pore over the files Tasha had sent.

Images of the goat mask flashed on her screen, its coarse, grotesque features both familiar and haunting. But it wasn't the mask that caught her attention—it was the material embedded in its seams. The fibers were soaked in a residue matching the mystery substance found in the barrels. Whatever it was, it wasn't natural.

Amy leaned back in her seat, letting her mind wander. The trident symbol gnawed at her thoughts. It wasn't just a mark—it was a message. Someone wanted to make sure they were seen, but why? And what did the ocean have to do with it?

Portland Field Office

By the time Amy arrived at the field office in Portland, the rain was coming down in sheets, the city a blur of gray and green under the stormy sky. The air here felt heavier, charged with an unease she couldn't shake.

Tasha was waiting for her in the evidence room, surrounded by photographs, files, and samples. She gestured to a monitor displaying images of the trawler and its grim contents.

"This is everything we've got so far," Tasha said, handing Amy a pair of gloves. "Take a look."

Amy inspected the goat mask first, her gloved fingers tracing its edges. The material was damp, reeking of salt and decay. The fibers matched what she'd seen in Seattle, but the residue was denser here, almost oily.

"The barrels," she said, moving to the next table. "What's in them?"

Tasha sighed. "A toxic cocktail of pollutants. The lab identified traces of crude oil, industrial solvents, and something … synthetic. We're still trying to figure out what it is. But the skeletal remains—those were a surprise."

Amy's breath caught. "Any idea who they belong to?"

"Not yet," Tasha said. "But the bones show signs of exposure to extreme heat and pressure, like they were compressed with the waste."

Amy's jaw tightened. The level of disregard for human life was staggering.

"Who owned the trawler?" Amy asked, moving to the next table where the manifest was spread out.

"The company's a shell," Tasha said. "Registered in the Cayman Islands. We're digging, but so far, nothing concrete. It's the trident symbol that's throwing us off. It's not tied to any known cartel or trafficking ring."

Amy stared at the symbol etched into the metal, her mind racing. "Then we're looking at someone new. A group or individual operating in the shadows, leaving just enough breadcrumbs to taunt us."

A Call from Her Mother

As the day wore on, Amy stepped outside for a moment of air, the drizzle misting her red hair. She reached into her coat pocket to pull out her phone, only to see several missed calls from her mother.

With a sigh, she dialed back.

"Amy, dear!" her mother's voice came through, warm but laced with worry. "We haven't heard from you in days. Your father's convinced you're drowning in work again."

"I'm fine, Mum," Amy said softly, leaning against the damp brick wall of the field office. "It's just been busy."

"Busy saving the world, I suppose," her mother said, a smile in her voice. "Just don't forget to take care of yourself, love. You're no good to anyone if you burn out."

Amy closed her eyes, letting the familiar comfort of her mother's voice wash over her. "I'll be careful, I promise."

"And don't forget your da," her mother added. "He's been pacing by the lake all morning, convinced you've forgotten about us entirely."

Amy chuckled despite herself. "I could never forget. Tell him I'll call soon."

The Ocean's Call

While night fell, Amy returned to the evidence room, the weight of the case pressing down on her. The oceans were screaming for help, their once-pristine waters poisoned by greed and cruelty.

She stared at the trident symbol one last time before pulling out her laptop. Whoever was behind this, they'd made a mistake leaving so many clues. By daybreak, surveillance footage filled her screen, each pixel a potential lead. Amy stared at the trident symbol, the edges of the carving rough and deliberate, as though someone had etched it with rage or conviction. It was a mark of power, but also of warning—an ancient call that transcended time and geography. Whatever this was, it wasn't just criminal; it was deeply symbolic.

The rain outside the field office window had turned into a steady downpour, streaking the glass and turning the world into a canvas of gray. Amy's mind raced with possibilities as she cross-referenced files on her laptop, mapping the connections between Seattle, Portland, Henderson, Diego, and now, this enigmatic symbol.

Her team was spread thin across the Pacific Northwest, piecing together clues while Amy juggled the weight of two fronts—the polluted oceans crying for salvation and the grim trail of mutilated bodies tied to this case.

She was interrupted by the sound of her phone buzzing again. It was Rivera, back in Atlanta.

"Lyons, you need to hear this," Rivera said without preamble. "We just got a report from the lab. The synthetic substance found in the barrels? It's a polymer blend used in military-grade bioplastics—something way out of the scope of any ordinary trafficking ring."

Amy's heart sank. "Military-grade? Are you saying this is government-backed?"

"I'm saying it's possible," Rivera replied. "Or, at the very least, someone with deep pockets and access to restricted materials. We're still digging, but it's not looking good."

Amy clenched her jaw, her fingers gripping the phone tightly. "Keep me updated. I'm following the Portland lead, but I'll need all the data you have on this. If Henderson and Diego are tied to something bigger, we need to know who's pulling the strings."

"Will do," Rivera said, then hesitated. "And, Amy … be careful. This is getting dangerous."

Amy hung up and stared at her reflection in the rain-streaked window. She could feel it, too—the shift in the air, the unease creeping into her every move. This wasn't just about solving a case anymore. It was about stopping something that threatened both humanity and the planet.

Later that night, Amy drove to the docks where the trawler was impounded. The rain had slowed to a drizzle, and the air smelled of salt and oil, heavy with the scent of industry. She parked her rented eco-friendly, 2025 Ford Mustang Mach E and stepped out while pulling her coat tighter against the damp chill.

The docks were eerily quiet, save for the soft lapping of waves against the hulls of the ships. Amy felt a shiver run through her—not from the cold but from something deeper. The ocean felt restless tonight, its whispers louder than usual, as if warning her of what was to come.

She approached the trawler, its massive frame looming in the dim light of the dock's floodlights. The trident symbol was still visible on the hull, a sinister reminder of the forces at play. Amy reached out to touch it, her fingers brushing the cold, wet metal.

In that moment, she felt it again—a shift in the air, a deep unease that made her stomach churn. The ocean was speaking to her, but its message was muddled, fragmented, like static on a radio.

Amy took a step back, her resolve hardening. Whatever this was, whoever was behind it, she would uncover the truth. And if Henderson and Diego were tied to this chaos, she would bring them down.

She turned and walked back to her SUV, the rain beginning to fall again in heavy drops. The road ahead was long and treacherous, but Amy had never been one to shy away from a fight—especially one for the planet she loved.

"Money flows to me easily, freely, and abundantly. I am open to receiving limitless prosperity, and I use my wealth to create joy, freedom, and positive impact."
—Paris D.

Chapter 14

SHADOWS OF BETRAYAL

Diego's car idled outside Akemi's oceanfront villa, its sleek, black exterior glinting under the moonlight. The hum of the engine was the only sound breaking the stillness of the Miami night. Diego sat in the driver's seat, his hands gripping the steering wheel as he wrestled with his thoughts.

He hadn't called. He hadn't planned this. He was just here, driven by some subconscious pull he couldn't explain. But he needed someone— someone who could make him feel less like a broken man.

Inside, Akemi stood at the window, watching the car. Her sharp eyes narrowed as she recognized the familiar silhouette.

Diego.

She let out a frustrated breath and tugged her silk robe tighter around her slender frame. *Of course, he would show up unannounced*, she thought bitterly. *Typical Diego. Always thinking he can just walk back in.*

She descended the marble staircase, her bare feet silent against the cool floor. When she opened the door, Diego's expression was a mix of guilt and desperation.

"What are you doing here?" she asked, her voice clipped.

Diego hesitated, the weight of her disapproval hitting him harder than he expected. "I just … I needed to talk to someone."

Akemi crossed her arms, leaning against the doorframe. "And I'm supposed to be that someone? After everything?"

"Akemi, please," Diego said, his voice low and strained. "I don't have anyone else."

Her jaw tightened, but she stepped aside, letting him in. "Fine. But don't expect me to roll out the red carpet."

The Conversation

Diego sank into the plush chair in the living room, running a hand through his hair. The opulent surroundings felt suffocating, the stark contrast to the chaos in his mind. Akemi didn't sit. She remained standing, her arms crossed as she watched him with a guarded expression.

"They killed her," Diego finally said, his voice cracking. "They killed Khloe. And it's my fault."

Akemi's eyes flickered, but she said nothing. Her silence stretched, heavy and uncomfortable.

"I didn't know where else to go," Diego continued. "You're the only one who—"

"Don't," Akemi interrupted, her tone sharp. "Don't sit there and act like I'm your safety net. Like I'm the one you run to when your life falls apart."

Diego looked up at her, startled by her anger. "Akemi—"

"No," she snapped, cutting him off. "You don't get to do this, Diego. You don't get to show up here, crying about Khloe, when you lied to me. You had her, and you had me. You tried to have it all, and now look where we are."

Diego flinched as her words hit him like a slap. "I didn't mean for any of this to happen."

"You never do," Akemi shot back. "But somehow, it always does."

She began pacing, her frustration bubbling over. "Do you even know how much I gave up for you? How much I sacrificed, thinking you actually cared? And all the while, you were playing house with Khloe."

Diego stood, his tone defensive. "It wasn't like that, Akemi. You don't understand—"

"I understand perfectly," she said, her voice icy. "You lied to me, Diego. Over and over again. And now Khloe's dead, and you're here looking for what? Forgiveness? Comfort?"

Diego's shoulders slumped. "I'm just trying to figure out who did this. She was pregnant, Akemi. She was carrying my child."

Akemi's stomach churned at his words, but she didn't let it show. Instead, she narrowed her eyes. "And you think I know something? Is that why you're here?"

Diego hesitated, the faintest flicker of doubt crossing his face. "No … I just thought—"

"You thought what?" Akemi challenged, stepping closer. "That I'd welcome you with open arms? That I'd help you piece your life back together after you tore mine apart?"

The room fell silent, the tension crackling like a live wire.

The Turning Point

Diego sighed, his voice softer now. "I'm sorry, Akemi. For everything. I know I messed up. I know I hurt you."

Akemi stared at him, her expression unreadable. For a moment, he thought she might forgive him, that the anger in her eyes might soften.

But then she turned away, her voice cold and detached. "Sorry doesn't bring Khloe back. It doesn't fix anything."

Diego stepped closer, his desperation mounting. "Akemi, please. I need your help. I need to figure out who did this."

Akemi's hands tightened into fists at her sides, but she kept her back to him. *You're looking at her*, she thought bitterly.

"I can't help you," she said aloud. "You need to leave."

Diego froze, her words cutting deeper than he expected. "Akemi …"

"Leave, Diego," she repeated, her voice firm. "Before I say something I can't take back."

Reluctantly, Diego nodded and walked toward the door. He hesitated before stepping out, glancing back at her one last time. "I'm sorry," he said again, his voice barely above a whisper.

Akemi didn't respond. She stood motionless, listening as the door closed behind him and his car engine faded into the night.

Once she was alone, Akemi collapsed onto the couch, her composure finally breaking. She buried her face in her hands, her breaths coming in shallow gasps.

Killing Khloe had been supposed to free her from Diego's hold, but it hadn't. If anything, it had tied her to him even more.

And now, he was digging, searching for answers. How long before he found out the truth?

Akemi looked up, her reflection in the glass window staring back at her, shadowed and fractured. She couldn't let Diego uncover her secret.

Not yet. Not until she was ready to end this for good.

While the waves crashed against the shore outside, Akemi made her decision. She would keep playing the role of the loving mother, the radiant goddess everyone admired. But beneath the surface, she would prepare for what was coming.

Because when Diego came back—and she knew he would—she would be ready. And this time, there would be no loose ends.

The Past Calls Back

Akemi stared out at the inky expanse of the ocean, the waves shimmering under the faint glow of the crescent moon. The sound of the crashing tide was usually soothing, but tonight, it was a cruel reminder of the storm brewing inside her. Her phone sat on the table, its screen dark and lifeless, though she found herself glancing at it every few minutes, waiting for something—or someone.

The room was dim, lit only by the soft amber glow of a single lamp. Her son, Dominic, was upstairs asleep, the faint sound of his nightlight's ocean waves machine barely audible over the real ones outside. Akemi brushed a strand of her curly hair behind her ear and sighed.

Just as she reached for her glass of wine, her phone buzzed violently against the table. The sound shattered the silence, making her flinch. She stared at the screen, her heart racing as an unknown number flashed across it.

Her first instinct was to ignore it—calls from unknown numbers rarely brought good news. But something about this felt different. Hesitating, she swiped to answer.

"Hello?" she said cautiously.

There was a pause on the other end, a crackling of static. Then a familiar voice, smooth and deep, filled her ear.

"Damn, Akemi. You sound like you've seen a ghost."

Akemi froze, the glass slipping from her fingers and shattering on the floor. She didn't even notice the shards as she gripped the phone tighter, her breath caught in her throat.

"Zeke?" she whispered, her voice trembling.

A low chuckle rumbled through the line. "The one and only."

Her mind raced. *Zeke? Out of jail? How?* The last she'd heard, he was locked up, with no chance of parole. And yet, here he was, calling her like no time had passed.

"You—you're out?" she stammered, her voice a mixture of shock and relief.

"Miss me already?" Zeke teased, his tone lighter than she expected.

Akemi couldn't help but let out a shaky laugh, the tension in her chest loosening just slightly. "Don't flatter yourself."

"Too late," Zeke shot back. "But yeah, I'm out. Thought I'd surprise you."

Akemi sank onto the couch, her legs suddenly weak. "Zeke, how? When? Does anyone else know?"

"Long story," Zeke replied, his voice taking on a more serious tone. "But let's just say I had some help from the right people. And no, nobody else knows—not yet."

Akemi bit her lip, her thoughts spiraling. "Why are you calling me, Zeke?"

"Because," Zeke said, his voice softening, "you're the only one I trust right now. And … I needed to hear your voice."

The vulnerability in his words caught her off guard. Zeke was usually so guarded, so composed. This side of him was rare, and it tugged at something deep inside her.

"Well," she said, forcing a smirk to her lips, "you've got a funny way of making an entrance. No postcard, no carrier pigeon, just a creepy late-night call?"

Zeke laughed, the sound warm and genuine. "What can I say? I like to keep you on your toes."

The Conversation Deepens

While they talked, Akemi found herself relaxing, the weight of the evening temporarily lifting. Zeke was the only person who truly knew her—the real her, not the polished, radiant version she showed to the world.

"I heard about Khloe," Zeke said suddenly, his voice cutting through the lighthearted banter. "I'm sorry."

Akemi's smile faltered. "Yeah," she said quietly. "It's been … a lot."

"She didn't deserve that," Zeke added. "And neither did you."

Akemi swallowed hard, her throat tight. She didn't know how to respond.

"Who do you think did it?" Zeke asked after a moment.

Akemi hesitated, her fingers tightening around the phone. "I don't know," she lied, her voice barely above a whisper.

Zeke was silent for a moment, as though weighing her words. "You sure about that?"

Her heart skipped a beat. "What's that supposed to mean?" she asked, her tone sharper than she intended.

"Relax," Zeke said, though his voice carried a hint of suspicion. "I'm just saying—you've always been good at figuring things out. If anyone can get to the bottom of this, it's you."

Akemi exhaled, her grip on the phone loosening. "Yeah," she said softly. "Maybe."

As the call wound down, Zeke's tone shifted again, a playful edge creeping back into his voice.

"By the way," he said, "you owe me a drink."

Akemi raised an eyebrow, her lips twitching into a small smile. "Oh, do I?"

"Yeah," Zeke replied. "For making me worry about you all these years. You've got some nerve, Akemi."

She laughed, the sound light and genuine. "You're impossible, Zeke."

"And you love it," he shot back.

Akemi shook her head, a faint blush coloring her cheeks. "Goodnight, Zeke."

"Goodnight, Akemi. Stay out of trouble."

The call ended, and Akemi sat in silence, the sound of the waves filling the room once more. She stared at the phone in her hand, her mind a whirlwind of emotions.

Zeke was out. The one person who could see through her facade, who knew her darkest secrets, was back in her life.

And as much as it terrified her, a small part of her felt relief. Because if anyone could help her navigate the chaos she'd created, it was Zeke.

But she also knew that his return would only complicate things further. Secrets had a way of surfacing, and with Zeke back in the picture, it was only a matter of time before everything unraveled.

For now, though, she allowed herself a small smile as she gazed out at the ocean.

"Zeke," she murmured to herself, shaking her head. "You've got a hell of a way with timing."

Akemi sat in the dim light of her living room, her thoughts swirling like the restless waves outside her window. The phone call from Zeke had left her both shaken and strangely comforted. His return was a reminder of who she truly was—both the parts she embraced and the parts she tried desperately to hide.

She stood and walked to the shattered wine glass still lying on the floor. The jagged edges glinted in the warm light, a perfect metaphor for her life: fragile, broken, and dangerous to touch. Carefully, she gathered the pieces, placing them in the trash.

As she stood upright again, her gaze lingered on her phone. A new worry tugged at her—a worry she hadn't let herself fully acknowledge until now. It had been three weeks since she last heard from Miami, and while their communication was sporadic at best, Miami always had a way of resurfacing when Akemi needed her most.

Grabbing her phone, she pulled up Miami's contact and pressed the call button. The line rang once, then twice, and eventually cut to voicemail.

"This is Miami. Leave it. Or don't," came Miami's familiar but curt voice, followed by the tone.

Akemi hesitated before leaving a message. "Hey, it's me. Call me back when you can … It's important." She paused, her voice softening. "Zeke's out."

She ended the call and stared at the screen, her stomach twisting with unease. Miami had been like a sister to her, someone who knew every corner of her life—the beautiful and the ugly. Not being able to reach her now, when everything was unraveling, made her feel more alone than ever.

The Suspicious Shadow

Just as she set the phone down, a flicker of movement outside the window caught her eye. Her body tensed, every nerve on high alert. For a moment, she thought she was imagining it, but then she saw it again—a shadow shifting just beyond the porch.

Akemi's heart pounded as she moved silently toward the front door. Her hand hovered over the knob before she slowly turned it, stepping out into the cool night air. The breeze carried the faint scent of salt and seaweed, and the sound of waves crashing against the shore filled her ears.

"Who's there?" she called out, her voice steady despite the unease coursing through her.

Silence. Only the wind and the waves answered.

With a frown, Akemi stepped further onto the porch, scanning the darkness for any sign of movement. Nothing. She let out a slow breath, trying to calm her racing heart.

"Get a grip," she muttered to herself, shaking her head.

As she turned to go back inside, a faint sound stopped her in her tracks—a low, almost imperceptible laugh. It was distant but unmistakable, and it sent a chill down her spine.

Akemi froze, her eyes narrowing as she peered into the shadows. She clenched her fists, her mind racing with possibilities.

"Keep playing games," she muttered under her breath. "You'll regret it."

The Worry Deepens

Back inside, she locked the door, double-checking the bolt. Her hand lingered on the doorknob for a moment before she pulled away, heading upstairs to check on Dominic.

Her son was still fast asleep, his tiny chest rising and falling in rhythm with the waves outside. The sight of him brought a small, fleeting sense of peace, but it wasn't enough to dispel the unease lingering in her chest.

In her bedroom, she grabbed her phone again and stared at the call log. Miami's name was still at the top, and she debated trying again. Instead, she sent a text: *Where are you? Call me back. Please.*

The silence on the other end felt heavier than before. Akemi climbed into bed, pulling the covers up while she stared at the ceiling.

Zeke's sudden reappearance, Miami's uncharacteristic silence, and the shadow outside—it was all too much.

The laugh echoed in her mind, and for a moment, she considered the possibility that her paranoia was getting the best of her. But her instincts, sharpened by years of survival, told her otherwise.

Someone was watching.

Something was coming.

And Akemi wasn't sure if she'd be ready for it when it arrived. She felt a chill run down her spine, a harbinger of a storm brewing on the horizon. Outside, the wind picked up, rattling the windows with a force that mirrored the turmoil within her.

Chapter 15
THE TWIN FLAMES

The Aston Martin DBX 707 hummed down the coastal highway as Diamond's fingers tightened on the steering wheel. The coordinates from the cryptic note burned in her mind, and as much as she wanted to dismiss it as just another riddle in her chaotic life, there was something about the man who had given it to her that she couldn't shake.

It wasn't just the way he slipped the note through her car window at the gas station two days ago—calm, deliberate, almost reverent. It was the look in his eyes. For a brief second, their gazes had locked, and she felt something unfamiliar: a quiet warmth that tugged at the edges of her guarded heart.

Diamond wasn't the type to let strangers leave an impression. Her world was too sharp, too dangerous for sentiment. But now, as she drove toward an unknown destination with nothing but a set of coordinates and her instincts, she found herself replaying that moment.

"Get a grip, Diamond," she muttered to herself, brushing a strand of her glossy black hair from her face.

Her Aston Martin sped over the winding road, the cliffs falling away to the ocean below. The setting sun cast a golden glow over the waves, and the salty breeze teased through the cracked window, tangling with her thoughts.

Diamond and Paris:
2013

The note in her pocket reminded her of the moment she first met Paris in 2013. The two of them were polar opposites then—Diamond with her razor-sharp intellect and no-nonsense demeanor, Paris with her fearless charisma and wild ambition.

It was a chance meeting in Monaco, during a glitzy charity auction where high rollers gathered to flaunt their wealth. Diamond had been there on business, scouting potential clients for a high-profile tech security firm she was building. Paris had been there for a different kind of business: running cons on the elite to fund her growing empire.

The two had crossed paths at the bar, where Diamond caught Paris in the middle of a con. A lesser woman might have exposed her. Diamond? She offered to help.

"I've been watching you work," Diamond had said, her tone cool but tinged with admiration.

Paris raised a perfectly arched brow, her red lips curling into a smirk. "And?"

"And you're sloppy with your timing," Diamond replied bluntly. "That guy? He's going to realize his watch is missing the second you walk away. But if you're smart, you'll leave it on the table and let him think he misplaced it."

Paris studied her for a long moment, then laughed—a rich, unapologetic sound. "You're bold. I like that. What's your name?"

"Diamond," she said simply.

From that night on, the two became inseparable. They didn't just work together; they built an empire. Paris handled the charm, the deals, and the dirty work, while Diamond ran the logistics, the tech, and the strategy. Together, they were unstoppable.

Present Day

Diamond shook off the memory as she approached the estate. The sun dipped below the horizon, leaving the cliffs bathed in twilight. The house loomed ahead, shrouded in shadows that seemed to breathe with the wind.

She parked the Aston Martin in the gravel driveway, her heart racing with a mix of anticipation and unease. The man at the gas station had felt like a ghost from a past she couldn't remember, but now, standing before the door of this mysterious property, she felt like she was stepping into a future she couldn't predict.

She pushed the door open cautiously, her green eyes scanning the dimly lit interior. The scent of salt and aged wood filled her nose, and the faint sound of waves crashing below echoed through the space.

Diamond's heels clicked softly against the wooden floors as she made her way into the grand foyer. Her fingers brushed the note in her coat pocket, the words running through her mind like a mantra.

Sometimes, the past comes calling when you least expect it.

She glanced toward the staircase, her heart pounding. She couldn't explain it, but something about this place felt tied to the man who had given her the note. She didn't know his name, his intentions, or why he had chosen her. But she knew one thing: She wasn't leaving without answers.

Diamond took a deep breath as she ascended the staircase of the mysterious estate. Her hand trailed along the polished wood banister, her mind a storm of unanswered questions. The air inside the house was thick with mystery, but her thoughts pulled her back to a simpler time—a moment when life wasn't riddled with secrets and danger but instead filled with possibility.

Flashback to 2014

The scene unfolded in slow motion: Monaco again, but this time on the open road. The late afternoon sun cast golden streaks over the azure coastline, the salty wind whipping through Diamond's long black hair. She sat in the passenger seat of a sleek white Lamborghini Aventador, her hand resting on the window frame as the engine roared beneath them.

Paris, in the driver's seat, her signature red lipstick gleaming in the sunlight, wore oversized black sunglasses that reflected the road ahead. Her curly caramel hair spilled over her shoulders, wild and carefree, matching the energy in her radiant hazel eyes. She pressed her foot down harder on the pedal, a mischievous grin spreading across her face.

Diamond laughed, a sound that was rare for her but entirely unrestrained in that moment. "You're insane, you know that?" she shouted over the roar of the engine and the wind tearing through the cabin.

"And you love it!" Paris shot back, her voice dripping with confidence. She cranked up the music—a pulsing beat of a K.Mitchell house track Million Hearts made the air between them feel electric.

Ahead, the winding coastal road beckoned, but Paris didn't slow down. She lived for moments like this, where the world blurred around her, where freedom felt like a tangible thing she could grab with both hands.

The Lamborghini screeched to a halt at the crest of a hill, overlooking the sparkling Mediterranean. Paris threw the car into park and leapt out, her laughter echoing as she held her arms out wide.

"This!" she exclaimed, spinning in place as her flowy white jumpsuit caught the breeze. "This is what we live for, Diamond! The power, the freedom, the world at our feet!"

Diamond stepped out more composed, smoothing her black silk blouse and designer trousers. Her emerald eyes, usually sharp and calculating, softened as she watched her best friend soak in the moment.

"You're ridiculous," Diamond said, but a smile tugged at the corner of her lips.

Paris turned to her, her expression suddenly serious but no less passionate. "Ridiculous? Babe, this is destiny. You and me, we're untouchable. No one can do what we do."

Diamond's smile grew wider. "Then let's do it. Let's take everything this world owes us."

Paris grinned, her energy contagious. She grabbed Diamond's hand and spun her in a carefree dance, their laughter carried off by the wind.

It was a memory Diamond held close to her heart—a moment of pure freedom, untainted by the chaos that would come later. Back then, they were just two women with sharp minds, beauty that turned heads, and an unshakable bond. They were unstoppable, and they knew it.

Back to the Present

Diamond snapped back to reality as her heels reached the top of the staircase. The house was silent, save for the occasional creak of wood beneath her steps. She pressed a hand to her chest, feeling her heart steady after the flash of memory.

For a moment, she allowed herself a small smile. That carefree version of her still existed, buried beneath layers of responsibility and danger. And Paris? Paris was still that unstoppable force of nature, somewhere out there, likely causing trouble and winning at it.

But now, Diamond had her own mission. The note, the man, the coordinates—they were all pieces of a puzzle she was determined to solve.

She squared her shoulders and pushed open the door at the end of the hall, ready to face whatever lay ahead.

Chapter 16
STORM WARNINGS

Dream adjusted her emerald-green blazer, its sleek fabric shimmering faintly under the soft glow of the chandelier in her downtown Atlanta penthouse. The rain outside lashed against the floor-to-ceiling windows, the city lights blurred by streaks of water. She sipped her glass of red wine, her sharp almond-shaped eyes scanning the skyline with quiet intensity. Her auburn curls were pinned into a neat bun, giving her an air of power and control—though inside, her mind raced with chaos.

Her husband, Brandon, stood by the kitchen counter, absentmindedly scrolling through his phone. His tall frame leaned casually against the marble, his tailored shirt open at the collar. He had the kind of effortless confidence that made him magnetic. But tonight, his usual charm was subdued, replaced by an undercurrent of tension.

"I got a call today," Brandon said, breaking the silence. His deep voice was steady, but there was a weight behind it.

Dream glanced over her shoulder, her perfectly arched brows lifting in curiosity. "From who?"

"Someone asking questions about Zeke."

Dream froze for a split second before resuming her sip of wine, masking her reaction. "Zeke? What about him?"

Brandon frowned. "They didn't say much. Just that his name is starting to come up in circles it shouldn't. And with Mr. Henderson still out for blood …"

Dream set her glass down, walking over to Brandon with calculated steps. Her heels clicked softly against the hardwood floor. "You don't have to worry about Zeke," she said, placing a hand on his chest. "He's always been a survivor."

"That's not the point," Brandon said, his tone sharpening. "If Henderson is sniffing around, it won't stop with Zeke. It'll come back to us, Dream. You know that."

She smiled, but it didn't reach her eyes. "Let me handle it."

Brandon studied her for a moment, his dark eyes narrowing. "Dream, what aren't you telling me?"

She shook her head, stepping away. "Nothing you need to know right now."

"Dream—"

Her phone buzzed on the counter, cutting him off. Dream grabbed it quickly, the name on the screen making her heart skip: *Private Number.*

"I need to take this," she said, already walking toward the study.

"Dream!" Brandon called after her, but she was already gone, shutting the door firmly behind her.

Dream's Secret Plan

In the privacy of her study, Dream sank into the leather chair and answered the call. "What do you have for me?"

A voice on the other end responded, low and clipped. "We've got eyes on Henderson's men. They're moving north, likely to regroup. You want us to follow?"

"Yes," Dream said without hesitation. "And I want every detail about their movements. I don't care how long it takes or how much it costs."

"You got it."

The call ended, and Dream leaned back, exhaling slowly. She unlocked the hidden drawer in her desk and pulled out a manila folder marked *Henderson.* Inside were pages of intel she'd been gathering for months—names, addresses, financials.

Brandon thought she was just trying to protect their family, but Dream had bigger plans. Plans that would end Mr. Henderson once and for all. She had connections—powerful ones—and she wasn't afraid to use them.

But there was another reason she couldn't let Brandon know the full truth: Zeke.

The memory of the last time she'd seen him flashed in her mind. It was late at night, and he'd shown up at her front door, pale and shaking. She'd let him in, thinking he was hurt, but what she saw terrified her.

Flashback

Zeke sat in her living room, his bronze dreadlocks tangled and his hazel-green eyes wild. Sweat dripped down his face as he clutched his head.

"Zeke, what's going on?" Dream asked, kneeling in front of him.

"I—I can't control it," he stammered, his voice trembling.

Before she could ask what he meant, strange objects began to rise around the room: a vase, a lamp, even a chair. Dream stumbled back, her eyes widening.

"Zeke!" she shouted. "What the hell is happening?"

"I don't know!" he screamed, his panic making the objects spin faster.

Dream could only watch in horror as Zeke collapsed to the floor, gasping for breath. The objects crashed down around him one by one.

When it was over, Zeke looked up at her, his face pale and tears streaming down his cheeks. "Don't tell anyone, Dream. Please. Not even Brandon."

She nodded, still shaken but determined to protect him. "I've got you, Zeke. Always."

Back to the Present

Dream shook off the memory, her heart pounding. She had no idea what Zeke was capable of, but she knew one thing for certain: Mr. Henderson would stop at nothing to destroy him. And if that happened, she and Brandon wouldn't be safe, either.

Her phone buzzed again, this time with a text from an unknown number: *You're running out of time. Make your move.*

Dream's jaw clenched as she stared at the message. She wasn't just protecting herself anymore—she was playing a dangerous game, and the stakes were higher than ever.

She stood, straightening her blazer and walking back to the living room. Brandon looked up from his phone, concern etched on his face.

"Everything okay?" he asked.

Dream forced a smile. "Everything's fine," she lied. I'm going to the study to look through a couple files before dinner. I'll just be a minute." He said nothing! He gave a simple head nod!

But deep down, he knew the storm was just beginning.

The air felt electric with tension, each moment ticking away like a countdown to chaos.

Dream stood in her study, staring at the drawer where she kept the manila folder on Henderson. Her gaze drifted to a smaller compartment below, one that held something even more personal. With a soft click, she slid it open and pulled out a leather-bound notebook.

Inside were pages of numbers, carefully written in Zeke's unmistakable handwriting. She flipped through them, her fingers brushing over the codes, amounts, and instructions. The stash of cash he'd left her all those years ago had been the foundation for everything she'd built since.

Dream's move into her luxurious penthouse wasn't the result of Brandon's income or some lucky investment. It was Zeke's gift—a safety net he'd secretly left behind when he vanished from her life.

At the time, she didn't know what to make of it. The money came with no note, no explanation, just a quiet assurance that he had her back. She'd told no one, not even Brandon, about where it came from. And now, with Zeke back in the picture, she wondered if he'd left it knowing she might one day need it to protect herself from the same dangers that haunted him.

"Always thinking ten steps ahead," she murmured to herself, closing the notebook.

Livingroom Revelations

Dream walked back into the living room where Brandon sat, flipping through channels on the TV. He barely looked up as she sank into the plush couch across from him, but the tension between them lingered.

"You've been quiet all night," Brandon said, setting the remote down.

Dream shrugged, swirling the wine in her glass. "Just a lot on my mind."

"About Zeke?" he pressed.

Her eyes snapped to his, but she quickly recovered, giving a dismissive laugh. "No, about the Henderson situation. You're the one who brought him up earlier, remember?"

Brandon leaned forward, his elbows on his knees, studying her carefully. "Dream, if there's something you're not telling me—"

A loud *ding* interrupted him. Dream's phone lit up on the coffee table, and her heart sank when she saw the name on the screen: *Zeke*.

Brandon glanced at the phone, his brow furrowing. "Who's that?"

"No one important," Dream said quickly, snatching the phone and heading back toward the study. "I'll be right back."

The Call From Zeke

Once she was safely behind the study door, Dream answered the call.

"Zeke," she said, her voice sharp. "You can't just call me like this."

"Relax," Zeke said, his voice calm but tinged with urgency. "I'm not calling to make your life harder."

"You being out of jail already did that," Dream shot back, pacing the room. "Do you have any idea what kind of heat is on me and Brandon because of you?"

"I didn't call to talk about Brandon," Zeke said bluntly.

Dream froze, gripping the phone tighter. "Then why are you calling?"

"I left you that stash for a reason, Dream," he said, his tone softening. "I knew one day you'd need it to protect yourself. But now … now I'm the one who needs you."

Her breath hitched. "Zeke, you don't understand what you're asking."

"Yes, I do," he replied. "Henderson's coming for me, Dream. And when he does, he's coming for anyone I've ever cared about. That includes you."

Dream leaned against the desk, her mind racing. "What do you want me to do?"

"Stay ready," Zeke said simply. "And keep an eye on Brandon."

"What does Brandon have to do with this?" she asked, her voice rising.

But Zeke didn't answer. The line went dead, leaving Dream staring at the phone in disbelief.

Brief Flashback

As Dream sat in the silence of her study, a memory from years ago came rushing back. She was standing in an empty warehouse, the air thick with the scent of oil and metal. Zeke had just handed her a duffel bag filled with cash.

"What's this for?" she'd asked, frowning.

"Insurance," Zeke had said, his hazel-green eyes locking onto hers. "In case I ever can't be there for you."

Dream had wanted to argue, to tell him she didn't need his money, but something in his voice stopped her. There was a finality to it, like he knew this might be the last time they saw each other.

"Just promise me one thing," he'd said, his voice barely above a whisper.

"What?"

"Don't ever let anyone take away what's yours. Not Henderson. Not anyone."

Back to the Present

Dream snapped out of the memory as Brandon knocked on the door. "Everything okay?" he called.

"Yeah," she said, clearing her throat. "Just a work call."

She put the phone down and took a deep breath. If Zeke was right, then the storm brewing around them was far bigger than she'd anticipated. And if Henderson really was coming for them, she'd have to make a choice: Stay loyal to the life she'd built with Brandon, or stand by Zeke and the secrets they shared.

But one thing was certain—Dream wasn't going down without a fight.

Chapter 17

STORMS AND SECRETS

The rain fell in thick sheets over Atlanta, washing the city in a veil of gray. Mr. Henderson sat in the back of his limousine, the faint hum of jazz playing through the car's speakers. He swirled a glass of whiskey in his hand, staring out at the blurred city lights.

His nephew, Diego, sat across from him, his face a mixture of frustration and unease.

"You're distracted," Henderson said, his voice calm but carrying an edge of authority.

Diego shifted in his seat. "It's nothing I can't handle."

Henderson smirked, his dark eyes narrowing. "I don't pay you to handle 'nothing.' I pay you to ensure loose ends don't exist. And yet, here we are. Zeke out of prison. Dream and her husband slipping through the cracks. Even your own secrets, Diego—secrets have a way of becoming liabilities."

Diego clenched his jaw, gripping the edge of his seat. He wanted to retort, but he knew better than to cross Henderson in this mood.

"Uncle," Diego began, his voice measured. "I'll take care of Zeke. And anyone connected to him."

Henderson leaned forward, his glass resting on his knee. "You'd better. Because if you don't, Diego, I'll find someone who will. Blood ties only go so far in my world."

Diego nodded, his stomach knotting. He knew Henderson's threats weren't empty.

Dream and Brandon

Across town, Dream stood on the balcony of her penthouse, staring at the city below. The rain had let up, leaving the streets shimmering under the glow of streetlights. She wrapped her arms around herself, her mind racing with thoughts of Zeke, Henderson, and the secrets she'd buried so deeply.

Brandon walked up behind her, placing a hand on her shoulder. "You've been quiet all day."

"I'm fine," Dream replied, her voice distant.

Brandon frowned, stepping closer. "No, you're not. You're hiding something. Is it about Zeke? Or is it Henderson?"

Dream turned to face him, her expression unreadable. "It's about survival," she said cryptically.

Before Brandon could press further, Dream's phone buzzed on the nearby table. She picked it up and saw an unknown number flashing on the screen.

"Dream," the voice on the other end said, low and familiar.

Her breath caught. "Who is this?"

"You know exactly who," the voice replied. "We need to talk. Now."

Zeke in Hiding

Zeke hung up the phone, his heart pounding. He was holed up in a run-down motel on the outskirts of the city, the kind of place where no one asked questions. The faint flicker of a neon sign outside cast an eerie glow through the window.

He sat on the edge of the bed, his bronze dreadlocks falling over his face as he stared at a map spread across the mattress. On it were several circled locations—places tied to Henderson's operations.

Zeke's hazel-green eyes glimmered with determination. He wasn't just running anymore. He was planning.

But there was one location that stood out: a warehouse on the edge of the city, one that Henderson frequently used for his "business dealings."

"If I'm going to end this," Zeke muttered to himself, "it starts there."

Diego and Akemi

Meanwhile, Diego sat in his sleek black Maserati, parked outside Akemi's oceanfront property in Miami. He'd been there for nearly an hour, debating whether to knock on the door.

Inside, Akemi was pacing, her mind racing with thoughts of Zeke, Dream, and now Diego. She hadn't expected him to show up unannounced, and his sudden reappearance had thrown her off balance.

When she finally opened the door, Diego's expression was guarded, but his light skin and sharp features betrayed a flicker of uncertainty.

"We need to talk," he said simply.

Akemi crossed her arms, leaning against the doorframe. "About what? The lies you've been telling me? Or the fact that you're still wrapped up in Henderson's mess?"

Diego sighed, running a hand through his hair. "I'm trying to make things right, Akemi."

She scoffed. "You're always 'trying,' Diego. But somehow, you always leave a trail of destruction behind you."

Before Diego could respond, Akemi's phone buzzed. She glanced at the screen and saw Zeke's name. Her heart skipped a beat.

"You should go," she said abruptly, stepping back inside and closing the door.

A Mysterious Intersection

As the rain began to fall again, the paths of these interconnected lives seemed to spiral closer and closer. Dream stood on her balcony, clutching her phone. Zeke plotted his next move in his dimly lit motel room. Diego drove aimlessly through the city, his mind a whirlwind of guilt and anger. And Akemi stared at her phone, her finger hovering over the call button.

In the shadows, Henderson watched, his influence reaching farther than any of them realized.

The storm wasn't just brewing—it was here.

Chapter 18

PATHS COLLIDE

The storm rolled into Atlanta, thick clouds stretching across the sky like a bruise. Lightning cracked in the distance as if nature itself sensed the tension building among the tangled lives that fate had woven together.

Zeke stood in the shadows of a crumbling warehouse on the outskirts of the city, his breath fogging in the cold night air. He pulled his hood tighter around his face, scanning the area. He could feel the energy in the air—static, heavy, like a current running just beneath the surface.

His unique gift was a secret he kept guarded, but tonight, it was working overtime. He could sense the vibrations of the world around him—the hum of power lines, the faint scurrying of rats in the alley, even the subtle shift in the atmosphere that told him someone was watching.

"They're here," he muttered to himself, his hazel-green eyes glowing faintly under the flickering streetlights.

Dream and Brandon

Across town, Dream and Brandon were in their car, speeding toward the same warehouse. Dream's phone was clutched tightly in her hand, the message from Zeke still glowing on the screen:

Meet me where it all started. Come alone.

Brandon glanced over at her. "You're not seriously going to trust him, are you? The man can't stay out of trouble for five minutes."

Dream's jaw tightened. "Zeke saved my life more times than I can count, Brandon. If he says he needs me, I'm going."

Brandon sighed, gripping the wheel. "And dragging me along, of course."

Dream smirked despite herself. "You're my husband. You signed up for this."

As they approached the warehouse, Dream's expression grew serious. The tension in the air was palpable, the weight of unspoken secrets pressing down on them both.

Diego and Akemi

Diego pulled up outside the same warehouse in his Maserati, his mind racing. He had followed the breadcrumbs Zeke had been leaving, piecing together his trail. He wasn't sure why Zeke had chosen this place, but he knew one thing for certain: He needed answers.

Akemi wasn't far behind. She parked her car a block away, slipping into the shadows as she approached the building. Her heart raced as she thought about Zeke. The last time she'd seen him, he had been a broken man. But the Zeke she'd spoken to on the phone sounded different—stronger, more focused.

She didn't know what she would say when she saw him. But she knew she had to be there.

The Warehouse

The warehouse was a relic of Atlanta's industrial past, its rusted metal exterior riddled with graffiti and bullet holes. Inside, the air was thick with the scent of oil and decay.

Zeke stood in the center of the main room, his long bronze dreadlocks falling over his shoulders. He was calm, his hands in his pockets, but his mind was anything but. His psychic senses were firing on all cylinders, alerting him to every shift in the environment.

The sound of footsteps echoed through the space.

Dream and Brandon entered first, their faces a mixture of relief and wariness.

"Zeke," Dream said, her voice soft but steady. "What's going on?"

Before he could answer, another set of footsteps joined them. Diego emerged from the shadows, his expression dark and guarded.

"Funny seeing you here," Diego said, his voice dripping with sarcasm.

Dream's eyes narrowed. "Diego? What the hell are you doing here?"

Zeke raised a hand, silencing them both. "Wait."

The air shifted again. Zeke turned his head slightly, his hazel-green eyes locking onto the far side of the room.

"Akemi," he called out. "You can come out now."

There was a pause before Akemi stepped into the light. Her curly hair framed her face, her radiant energy at odds with the tension in her expression.

"Zeke," she said, her voice trembling slightly. "What is this? Why are we all here?"

Collision

Zeke stepped forward, his gaze sweeping over the group. "You're all here because of Henderson. He's been pulling strings for too long, and it's time we cut the cords."

Diego scoffed. "And what? You think we're all going to band together like some kind of team?"

Zeke's lips curved into a faint smile. "Something like that."

Dream crossed her arms. "You still haven't explained why you called us here, Zeke."

Zeke turned to her, his expression serious. "Because this isn't just about me anymore. Henderson isn't just coming for me—he's coming for all of us. And if we don't work together, none of us are going to make it out alive."

Akemi stepped closer, her voice low. "You think we can trust each other? After everything that's happened?"

Zeke met her gaze, his eyes glowing faintly. "We don't have to trust each other. We just have to trust that we all want the same thing: Henderson gone."

The group fell silent, the weight of Zeke's words sinking in.

A Mysterious Interruption

Before anyone could respond, the sound of tires screeching outside shattered the moment. Zeke's head snapped toward the entrance, his psychic senses screaming at him.

"They're here," he said, his voice low.

"Who's here?" Dream asked, panic creeping into her voice.

"Henderson's men," Zeke replied. "Get ready."

As the group scrambled to prepare, Zeke stood at the center of the room, his energy crackling around him like static electricity.

This was it. The collision of their lives, their secrets, and their futures. And the storm was just beginning.

The warehouse trembled with the hum of engines pulling up outside. Zeke's sharp gaze cut through the dim light, his posture stiffening. The others followed his line of sight, unease washing over them.

"Stay calm," Zeke said, his voice steady despite the chaos simmering beneath his skin. "They're here for me."

Dream's lips tightened. "Yeah? Well, they're going to have to go through all of us."

Diego chuckled darkly. "Brave words, but let's not get sentimental. If they're armed, we're toast."

Brandon raised a brow, his hands curling into fists. "Then I guess we better figure out who's running out first."

Zeke ignored the banter. Instead, he closed his eyes and reached out with his abilities, feeling the vibrations of the world around him.

The men outside weren't ordinary mercenaries; he could sense their disciplined movements, the measured breaths of trained killers.

"Four of them," Zeke murmured. "Three by the door, one circling the back."

Akemi tilted her head. "How the hell do you know that?"

"Just trust me," Zeke replied, opening his eyes. "Dream, Diego—stay by the side entrance. Brandon, cover the back. Akemi, you're with me."

Dream looked ready to protest but stopped when she saw the intensity in Zeke's expression. "Fine," she muttered. "But if you die on me, I'm kicking your ass in the afterlife."

Zeke smirked. "Deal."

The Attack

The first shot rang out like a crack of thunder, shattering the uneasy silence. Dream and Diego ducked behind a stack of crates as bullets ricocheted off the metal walls. Brandon slipped through the back exit, disappearing into the night.

Zeke moved with precision, guiding Akemi through the chaos. His senses flared as he anticipated the movements of their attackers, dodging bullets with almost unnatural grace.

"Zeke, what's your plan here?" Akemi shouted over the gunfire, her voice tinged with both fear and frustration.

"Survive," Zeke replied, his tone grim.

The attackers breached the warehouse, their masked faces illuminated by the flickering lights. Zeke lunged forward, disarming the first man with a swift strike. Akemi hesitated for a moment before grabbing a nearby metal pipe, swinging it at another attacker with surprising force.

Dream and Diego worked in tandem, their bickering momentarily set aside as they took down the men at the side entrance. Diego's movements were calculated, precise, while Dream fought with a ferocity born from years of loyalty to Zeke.

Brandon reappeared, dragging the unconscious body of the man who had circled the back. "One down," he announced, tossing the gun he'd confiscated onto the floor.

The Aftermath

The dust settled as the last attacker hit the ground. Zeke leaned against a support beam, his chest heaving. The others gathered around him, their faces a mix of relief and exhaustion.

"That wasn't just a random attack," Dream said, wiping sweat from her brow. "They knew we'd be here."

Zeke nodded, his jaw tightening. "Henderson's upping the ante. He's not just trying to scare us anymore—he's trying to take us out."

Diego crossed his arms, his expression dark. "So, what's the plan, genius? Because I don't know about you, but I'm not exactly keen on dying tonight."

Zeke glanced around the room, his hazel-green eyes scanning the faces of his unlikely allies. "The plan is simple. We stop running, and we start fighting back."

A Mysterious Call

Before anyone could respond, Zeke's phone buzzed in his pocket. He frowned as he pulled it out, his expression shifting from confusion to unease.

"It's an unknown number," he said, answering cautiously.

A distorted voice crackled through the line. "Zeke. You don't know me, but I know you. And if you want to survive, you'll listen carefully."

The group fell silent, tension thick in the air.

"Who is this?" Zeke demanded.

"That's not important," the voice replied. "What's important is that Henderson isn't your only enemy. There's someone else—someone pulling strings from the shadows."

Zcke's grip on the phone tightened. "What do you mean?"

"You'll find your answers in Miami, Florida. But be careful. Not everyone in your little group is who they seem."

The line went dead.

Revelations

Zeke lowered the phone, his mind racing.

"Who was it?" Akemi asked, her eyes narrowing.

"Someone who knows more than they're letting on," Zeke replied. "They said we need to go to Miami."

Dream groaned. "Of course it's Miami, Florida., Nothing good ever happens in Miami."

Diego smirked. "Says the woman who spent half her twenties partying there."

"Focus," Zeke snapped, cutting off the banter. "This isn't a game anymore. If we're going to survive, we need to figure out who's playing us—and why."

The group exchanged uneasy glances, the weight of their situation sinking in.

Outside, the storm began to subside, the rain washing away the blood and chaos of the night. But as the group prepared to leave, they all knew one thing for certain: The real storm was still ahead.

"I accept love and embody its pure essence. The divine synchrony of love echoes through my heart and soul, vibrating in perfect harmony with the universe."
—Paris D.

Chapter 19

PREPARATIONS AND UNEASY ALLIANCES

The safe house sat on the outskirts of the city, hidden behind dense trees and a winding dirt road. Inside, the group was scattered—some tending to injuries, others inspecting weapons and supplies. The air was thick with tension, and the hum of uneasy alliances buzzed louder than the fluorescent lights flickering above.

Akemi leaned against the far wall, arms crossed, watching Diego from the corner of her eye. He was seated at the table, cleaning his pistol with a precision that irritated her.

"You're really just going to sit there and pretend everything's fine?" she finally snapped, breaking the silence.

Diego looked up, his light eyes narrowing. "And what exactly do you want me to do, Akemi? Cry about it? Apologize for something I didn't do?"

"You didn't do?" Akemi's voice rose, her Trinidadian accent cutting through the room like a blade. "You lied to me, Diego. You tried to have your cake and eat it, too. Now, Khloe's dead, and we're cleaning up your mess."

The room went silent. Even Zeke, who had been pacing near the window, stopped and glanced at them.

"Can you two put this aside for five minutes?" Dream interjected, her tone sharp. "We've got bigger problems than your soap opera drama."

Akemi's eyes flashed, but she bit her tongue. She shifted her gaze to Zeke. "You really think this is a good idea? Bringing him along?"

Zeke sighed, running a hand through his bronze dreadlocks. "I don't like it, either, but we need him. Diego has connections—money, resources. If we're going to take on Henderson, we need every advantage we can get."

Akemi shook her head, clearly unconvinced. "Fine. But don't expect me to trust him."

Diego smirked, leaning back in his chair. "Trust is earned, Akemi. And if you give me the chance, I might just surprise you."

Supplies and Strategies

In the adjoining room, Brandon was organizing a collection of weapons and gadgets laid out on a metal table. Dream joined him, her brows furrowed as she inspected the arsenal.

"You think this is enough?" she asked, picking up a sleek black handgun.

Brandon shrugged. "It's not about having enough. It's about knowing how to use what you've got."

Dream rolled her eyes. "Thanks for the wisdom, Sun Tzu. I meant, do you think this is enough to take on Henderson?"

Brandon glanced at her, his dark eyes serious. "Nothing's ever enough when you're dealing with someone like him. But it's a start."

Zeke entered the room, his presence commanding immediate attention. "How's it looking?"

"We're set for now," Brandon replied, gesturing to the table. "Guns, ammo, a few surprises. But we're going to need more firepower if this thing escalates."

"It always escalates," Zeke muttered under his breath.

The Plan

The group gathered around the table, tension palpable. Zeke spread a map of Miami across the surface, marking several locations with a red pen.

"These are Henderson's known properties," he began, his tone steady and authoritative. "Warehouses, clubs, a couple of high-end restaurants he uses as fronts. If we're going to find out what he's planning, we need to start here."

Dream leaned over the map, her finger tracing one of the marked locations. "This one. It's his biggest nightclub, right? We hit it first."

"No," Zeke said firmly. "It's too obvious. He'll be expecting us there."

"So, what's the play?" Brandon asked.

"We start small," Zeke replied. "Hit one of the warehouses. Quietly. We gather intel, see what we're up against. Then, we move up the chain."

Diego chuckled, shaking his head. "You make it sound so simple."

"It's not," Zeke admitted. "But it's the only way."

A Quite Conversation

Later that night, as the others prepared to rest, Akemi found Zeke outside, leaning against the hood of a battered SUV. The night was cool, the stars obscured by a thin layer of clouds.

"Can't sleep?" she asked, her voice softer than before.

Zeke glanced at her, a faint smile tugging at his lips. "Too much on my mind."

Akemi stepped closer, crossing her arms against the chill. "You really think we can do this? Take him down?"

"I have to," Zeke said simply. "Henderson's not just a threat to me. He's a threat to everyone I care about."

Akemi studied him for a moment, her expression unreadable. "You're different, you know. Stronger. But … you're carrying something. Something heavy."

Zeke looked away, his jaw tightening. "I've always been carrying it. I just never realized how much it weighed."

Before Akemi could respond, Zeke turned to her, his hazel-green eyes piercing. "I know you don't trust Diego. Hell, I don't trust him, either. But right now, we need to focus. Can you do that?"

Akemi nodded slowly. "I can. For now."

Zeke gave her a small nod. "That's all I need."

A Moment of Humor

As they headed back inside, they passed Dream and Brandon, who were arguing over who would take the couch.

"You're bigger," Dream was saying, hands on her hips. "You'll fit on it better!"

"And you're smaller," Brandon countered. "You'll be more comfortable!"

Akemi chuckled, shaking her head. "You two sound like an old married couple."

Dream shot her a look. "Careful, Akemi. I might just start taking relationship advice from you."

Zeke smirked, the tension in his shoulders easing slightly. "Come on. We've got a long day tomorrow. Get some rest while you can."

While the group settled in for the night, the uneasy alliances and unresolved tensions lingered in the air. As, they mastered a game plan.

"I am rich and I get paid to exist."
—Paris D.

Chapter 20

YASMEEN JOINS THE FOLD

It was close to midnight when the unmistakable growl of an engine cut through the stillness surrounding the safe house. The group, already on edge, tensed as headlights illuminated the long driveway leading up to the property.

Zeke was the first to step outside, his hazel-green eyes narrowing against the beam of lights. He recognized the sleek black Rolls-Royce Cullinan immediately, its imposing frame a stark contrast to the modest vehicles parked around the house.

The driver's door opened, and Yasmeen stepped out with her signature elegance. Dressed in a tailored white suit that hugged her model-like frame, she exuded the kind of power and confidence that made everyone pause. Her long black hair cascaded down her back, and her emerald-green eyes, sharp and piercing, locked onto Zeke with a hint of amusement.

"Did someone forget to invite me to the party?" she teased, her Russian accent curling around the words like smoke.

Zeke couldn't help but smirk. "Yasmeen. I thought you had bigger fish to fry."

She tilted her head, her lips curving into a sly smile. "And miss all this chaos? Never."

Yasmeen's Entrance

Inside, the room fell silent as Yasmeen entered, her presence commanding attention. Akemi raised an eyebrow, already suspicious, while Dream and Brandon exchanged wary glances.

"Let me guess," Dream said, breaking the silence. "You're here to save the day?"

"Something like that," Yasmeen replied smoothly, her gaze sweeping over the group. She stopped at Zeke, her expression softening just enough for him to notice.

"Why are you really here, Yasmeen?" Zeke asked, leaning against the wall with his arms crossed.

Yasmeen reached into her designer bag and pulled out a sleek tablet. With a few taps, she projected a holographic map onto the wall, the image crisp and glowing. "Because you're all woefully underprepared," she said bluntly.

The map displayed several of Henderson's properties, but Yasmeen's version included layers of information the group hadn't uncovered yet—security details, supply chains, and even key personnel.

"How did you get all this?" Brandon asked, impressed despite himself.

Yasmeen smiled faintly. "Let's just say I have my ways. Henderson might think he's untouchable, but even he has cracks in his armor."

Tension in the Room

As Yasmeen explained her findings, Akemi leaned closer to Dream, whispering, "Who is she, exactly? She walks in here like she owns the place."

Dream smirked. "She might as well. That's Yasmeen Volkov—millionaire, genius, and, apparently, Zeke's biggest fan."

Akemi snorted. "Great. Another complication."

Meanwhile, Yasmeen continued her briefing, her tone cool and authoritative. But every now and then, her gaze would flicker toward Zeke, as if checking to see if he was impressed.

When she finished, Zeke stepped forward, his expression unreadable. "You didn't have to come all the way out here for this. You could've just sent the data."

Yasmeen shrugged, a glimmer of mischief in her eyes. "Maybe. But where's the fun in that?"

Work and Boundaries

Later, as the group dispersed to review Yasmeen's intel, she lingered in the corner with Zeke.

"You don't trust me," she said, more a statement than a question.

Zeke glanced at her, his bronze dreadlocks catching the dim light. "I trust you. I just don't know what you want."

Her emerald eyes softened. "What I want doesn't matter right now. What matters is taking down Henderson. After that … who knows?"

Zeke studied her for a moment, then nodded. "Thanks for coming, Yasmeen. We need all the help we can get."

She smiled, a rare, genuine smile. "Just try not to get yourself killed, okay? It would be … inconvenient."

Zeke chuckled, shaking his head. "I'll do my best."

Light Moment

As the night wore on, the group reconvened in the living room, where Yasmeen's map still glowed on the wall.

"So, what's the plan now?" Akemi asked, her tone clipped.

"We hit Henderson where it hurts," Zeke replied.

"Great," Akemi muttered. "And when that backfires, what's plan B?"

"Don't worry," Yasmeen interjected smoothly. "I have plenty of backup plans. And backup for the backup."

Brandon raised an eyebrow. "Is that supposed to make us feel better?"

Yasmeen smirked. "It should. I'm very thorough."

Dream leaned back in her chair, letting out a low whistle. "Well, aren't we lucky to have the queen of everything on our side?"

The group shared a rare laugh, the tension easing just slightly. But as the laughter faded, the weight of their mission settled back over them like a heavy blanket.

That night, as the group prepared for the next step, Zeke found himself on the porch, staring out at the dense forest surrounding the safe house. While he stood in silence, the moonlight filtering through the trees, a faint breeze carried the scent of rain. For a moment, it felt like the calm before the storm.

Chapter 21

BENEATH THE SURFACE

The safe house was quiet, save for the faint hum of insects outside and the occasional creak of floorboards as the others settled into their rooms. Zeke leaned against the porch railing, the cool night air brushing over his skin. His hazel-green eyes stared out into the darkness, but his mind churned with thoughts of the mission, of Henderson, and of the people depending on him.

The soft sound of footsteps pulled him from his thoughts. Yasmeen emerged from the doorway, her silhouette framed by the dim glow of the porch light. Her long black hair moved gently in the breeze, and for a moment, Zeke forgot everything else.

"Couldn't sleep?" he asked, his voice low.

"Sleep is overrated," Yasmeen replied, a small smile tugging at her lips. She stepped up beside him, her emerald-green eyes scanning the same horizon he had been lost in moments before.

They stood in silence for a moment, the weight of unspoken words heavy between them. Finally, Yasmeen broke the quiet.

"You don't have to do this alone, you know," she said, her tone softer than usual.

Zeke glanced at her, his expression unreadable. "I've been doing things alone for a long time. It's easier that way."

"Is it?" she countered, tilting her head to study him. "Or is that just what you tell yourself so you don't have to let anyone in?"

Zeke let out a low laugh, shaking his head. "You've got me all figured out, huh?"

Yasmeen smirked. "Not yet. But I'm working on it."

A Shared Burden

"You're good at this," Zeke said after a moment, his voice thoughtful.

"Good at what?" Yasmeen asked, turning to look at him.

"At deflecting," he replied. "You ask all the questions, but you never answer any."

She raised an eyebrow, a flicker of amusement in her gaze. "And what would you like me to answer, Zeke?"

He studied her for a long moment, as if searching for something in her expression. "Why are you here? Really. You don't need to be involved in this. You've got money, resources. You could walk away from all of this and still be fine."

Yasmeen's smile faded, and for the first time, her confident exterior cracked just slightly. "Maybe I could," she admitted. "But … I don't want to. Not when it matters this much."

"To me?" Zeke asked, his voice quiet.

"To all of us," she said quickly, though her eyes lingered on his. "You're not the only one who's lost people because of Henderson.

This fight—it's personal for me, too."

Zeke nodded slowly, his gaze dropping to the ground. "I get that. But you could still keep your distance."

"And let you get yourself killed?" she quipped, a faint smirk returning to her lips. "Not a chance."

An Unexpected Moment

The tension between them eased slightly, and Zeke let out a chuckle. "You've always been stubborn."

"And you've always been infuriating," Yasmeen shot back, though there was a playful edge to her tone.

For a moment, they both laughed, the sound cutting through the heavy atmosphere that had hung over the safe house all day.

But then, as the laughter faded, their eyes met again, and the air between them shifted.

"You're different, you know," Yasmeen said softly, her emerald eyes searching his.

"Different how?" Zeke asked, his voice just as quiet.

"You see things other people don't," she replied, her gaze steady. "You feel things ... deeply. It's rare."

Zeke looked away, a flicker of vulnerability crossing his face. "It's not always a good thing."

"No," Yasmeen agreed. "But it's what makes you ... you."

For a moment, Zeke didn't know how to respond. He wasn't used to people seeing him so clearly, and it unnerved him.

"You're dangerous, Yasmeen," he said finally, his voice tinged with humor.

"And you're frustrating," she countered, smirking.

"Guess we're stuck with each other, then," Zeke said, the corners of his mouth lifting in a small smile.

The Night Deepens

As the night grew colder, they stayed on the porch, their conversation drifting from strategy to lighter topics. Yasmeen shared a story about a botched mission in Monaco, complete with exaggerated hand gestures and a perfectly timed impression of the panicked team leader. Zeke, despite himself, couldn't stop laughing.

"You're insane," he said, shaking his head.

"Probably," Yasmeen replied, grinning. "But you like me anyway."

Zeke didn't respond, but the look in his eyes said enough.

When they finally retreated inside, the connection between them felt stronger, though unspoken. Yasmeen respected the boundaries Zeke had built, but there was no denying the quiet understanding growing between them.

As Zeke closed his door that night, he couldn't shake the feeling that Yasmeen was right: Maybe he didn't have to do this alone.

The Darkest Prison

Far from the safe house and the camaraderie Zeke was rediscovering, Autumn remained trapped in an isolated, sterile room. The walls were a stark, oppressive white, broken only by the faint hum of fluorescent lights above her. Her body felt heavy, her limbs unresponsive, bound to the hospital-style bed by thick leather straps.

The faint prick of another tranquilizer shot burned against her skin. Autumn's eyelids fluttered, her mind swimming in and out of consciousness, unable to fight the drug coursing through her veins.

In the corner of the room, a man in a goat head mask sat silently, watching. The grotesque mask had become a haunting symbol of Mr. Henderson's growing empire of fear.

A distant door creaked open, and Mr. Henderson stepped inside, his polished shoes clicking against the floor. His nephew, Diego, followed behind, his expression unreadable.

"How's our guest?" Henderson asked, his voice smooth, almost mocking.

"She's stable," the masked man replied.

"Good. We need her alive—for now," Henderson said, standing at the foot of Autumn's bed. He looked down at her, his face twisted into a smirk.

"I wonder," he mused, his tone dripping with cruelty, "what Zeke would do if he knew where you were. How far would he go? What would he give up?"

Diego shifted uncomfortably but said nothing. He didn't agree with everything his uncle did, but he was too deep in this game to back out now.

Henderson turned to leave but stopped in the doorway. "Keep her asleep. The longer she's under, the easier it'll be when we decide to … move her."

While the door shut behind him, Autumn's lips parted slightly, as if she were trying to speak. But no words came. Only the faint echo of her own thoughts, trapped in a drug-induced haze.

Back to the Safe House

Back at the safe house, Zeke sat on the edge of his bed, holding a worn photo of Autumn in his hands. Her smile in the picture was radiant, her eyes full of life. The memory of her voice, her laugh, her touch—it was the only thing keeping him grounded.

Unbeknownst to him, Yasmeen lingered outside his door, her usual confident demeanor softening. She could sense his pain, even though he tried to hide it.

She didn't knock, though. Zeke deserved his space, and Yasmeen respected that.

But as she turned to leave, she made a silent vow: No matter what it took, they would bring Autumn back.

Chapter 22
THE LONG GAME

The moon hung high over Miami, casting a silver glow on the city that pulsed with life even in the dead of night. But Zeke wasn't here to enjoy the view. From the window of Yasmeen's penthouse—a sprawling space overlooking the ocean—he stood in silence, his hazel-green eyes locked on the horizon.

"Diego's sweating," Yasmeen's voice broke the quiet, sharp and observant. She sat cross-legged on a sleek leather sofa, swirling a glass of aged whiskey in her hand.

"Good," Zeke replied, his tone measured. "He doesn't know it yet, but he's already done half the work for me."

Yasmeen arched a brow. "You're sure he's leading you to Autumn?"

"I'm not guessing," Zeke said, turning to face her. "When I ran into him at the warehouse, I caught her scent on him. That's not something he can fake."

Yasmeen's green eyes narrowed, her mind turning over the implications. "He's either directly involved or knows more than he's letting on."

"He knows," Zeke said, his voice hardening. "And he's going to slip up sooner or later."

Zeke's calm exterior masked the fire burning inside him. Autumn's scent, faint and fleeting as it was, had been enough to confirm she was alive. It was enough to ignite a resolve he hadn't felt in years.

The Miami Mission

The next morning, the team gathered around a holographic map projected on the penthouse coffee table. Yasmeen had spared no expense, equipping the group with state-of-the-art tech that only her vast resources could provide.

"All right, let's recap," Yasmeen began, her voice firm. "Diego has a meeting scheduled with a local contact tonight—someone who might be tied to Henderson's operation. If we play this right, we can use Diego to get closer to Henderson and Autumn."

"And if Diego catches on?" Just'n asked, leaning against the wall with his arms crossed. His hazel eyes glinted with intensity.

Zeke smirked, his bronze dreads brushing his shoulders as he tilted his head. "Diego won't catch on. He's too distracted by his own guilt."

"And what makes you so sure?" Yasmeen asked, though there was a hint of amusement in her tone.

"Because I've been feeding it," Zeke replied, his voice low but steady. "Every word, every look, every move—I've been planting seeds in his head. He thinks he's in control, but he's dancing to my tune."

The room fell silent for a moment as the weight of Zeke's words sank in.

"Well," Yasmeen finally said, a small, impressed smile playing on her lips, "remind me never to get on your bad side."

Diego's Next Move

Later that evening, Diego sat in a dimly lit bar near the Miami docks, nursing a glass of rum. The weight of his secrets pressed heavily on his chest. Zeke's presence had unsettled him, though he couldn't quite pinpoint why.

He pulled his phone from his pocket, hesitating before dialing Mr. Henderson. His uncle answered on the first ring.

"What is it?" Henderson's voice was curt, as always.

"We might have a problem," Diego admitted, lowering his voice. "Zeke's in Miami."

There was a pause, and when Henderson spoke again, his tone was icy. "If Zeke's there, it's because he's after something. Keep an eye on him—and don't screw this up."

Diego clenched his jaw, the reprimand stinging more than he cared to admit. "Yes, sir."

As he hung up, he felt a hand on his shoulder. He turned to see Zeke standing behind him, a calm but unreadable expression on his face.

"Didn't mean to interrupt," Zeke said, sliding into the seat across from him. "But we need to talk."

Diego swallowed hard, his instincts screaming that something wasn't right. But Zeke's disarming smile and steady gaze made it impossible to argue.

The Puppet Strings

What Diego didn't know was that Zeke had been monitoring him for days. He knew about the phone call to Henderson, and he knew Diego's guilt over Autumn's disappearance was eating him alive.

While the two men spoke, Zeke subtly pressed Diego for information, using his words like bait. Every time Diego tried to deflect, Zeke would steer the conversation back, his tone casual but firm.

"You're sweating again, Diego," Zeke finally said, leaning back in his chair.

Diego froze, his drink halfway to his lips.

"Relax," Zeke added, smirking. "I'm just saying—whatever's weighing on you, it's written all over your face."

Diego forced a laugh, but it sounded hollow.

"Look," Zeke continued, his tone softening just enough to seem sincere. "I get it. Life's messy. We all have things we wish we could undo. But the only way out is through, you know?"

Diego nodded slowly, his guard lowering just enough for Zeke to catch a glimmer of truth in his eyes.

And that was all Zeke needed.

Chapter 23
MIAMI HEAT

The sun glistened off the turquoise waters of Miami Beach, and the city buzzed with its signature blend of luxury and chaos. The team had set up shop in Yasmeen's private villa—a sprawling, glass-fronted masterpiece overlooking the ocean. Inside, the air hummed with tension as final preparations for the mission were underway.

Zeke stood in front of the mirror in a crisp white linen suit, its tailored lines hugging his tall, toned frame perfectly. A pair of sleek aviator sunglasses rested on his nose, and his bronze dreadlocks were tied loosely at the nape of his neck. The golden sunlight streaming through the villa's massive windows made his caramel complexion glow.

"You look like trouble," Yasmeen teased as she walked in, holding a pair of stilettos in one hand and a glass of champagne in the other.

Yasmeen was the embodiment of Miami chic. She wore a form-fitting emerald green dress that shimmered with every movement, highlighting her statuesque figure. Her long black hair cascaded down her back in soft waves, and her green eyes sparkled with mischief.

"I am trouble," Zeke shot back with a smirk.

Just'n entered next, adjusting the cuffs of his navy-blue blazer. The open-collared shirt underneath revealed just enough to make a statement. His polished leather loafers gleamed, and his confident stride matched the sharpness of his hazel gaze.

"This better be worth it," Just'n said, grabbing a drink from the bar. "I didn't put on this much cologne to leave empty-handed."

Mission Briefing

The group gathered around the glass dining table, where a 3D holographic map of Miami's port shimmered above a small projector. Yasmeen tapped a few buttons on her tablet, zooming in on a warehouse surrounded by shipping containers.

"This is the target," she said, her tone all business now. "Diego's meeting is happening here in less than two hours. He thinks it's just another transaction, but we'll be there to intercept."

"Security?" Zeke asked, his voice calm but sharp.

"Armed guards stationed at the entrance and perimeter," Yasmeen replied. "And at least three snipers on the surrounding rooftops."

"Sounds like a warm welcome," Just'n quipped, earning a chuckle from Yasmeen.

"We'll divide into two teams," Yasmeen continued. "Zeke and Just'n, you'll handle the ground team. I'll provide cover from the rooftop. Once we get the package—whatever Diego's exchanging—we'll rendezvous back here."

"And if things go south?" Just'n asked.

"They won't," Yasmeen said with a confident smile. "Because I've planned for everything."

The Setup

The villa's private garage roared to life as the team prepared to leave. Zeke slid into the driver's seat of a black Lamborghini Urus, its matte finish gleaming like a panther in the sunlight. Yasmeen followed in her crimson Ferrari Roma, the engine purring as she revved it for effect. Just'n, not one to be outdone, took the wheel of a silver Aston Martin DB11.

As they sped through Miami's bustling streets, the team synced their comms and ran through the plan one last time. The city's vibrant energy mirrored the adrenaline coursing through their veins.

"This is it," Zeke said over the comms as they approached the warehouse. "Showtime."

The Infiltration

The warehouse loomed ahead, its rusted walls hiding the secrets within. Yasmeen parked a few blocks away, scaling a nearby building with the agility of a trained assassin. From her vantage point, she had a clear view of the guards below.

"Snipers are in position," Yasmeen reported, her voice steady through the earpiece. "I've got eyes on all three."

"Good," Zeke replied. "Just'n, you're with me. Let's move."

The two men approached the warehouse on foot, blending into the shadows. Zeke's white suit might have been a bold choice, but he moved with the grace of a predator, his every step silent and deliberate. Just'n followed close behind, his eyes scanning for any sign of trouble.

As they reached the entrance, Zeke held up a hand to signal a pause. "Two guards. Ten o'clock," he whispered.

"On it," Yasmeen said. Moments later, two faint pops sounded through the comms, and the guards crumpled to the ground, tranquilizer darts protruding from their necks.

"Clear," Yasmeen confirmed.

Zeke and Just'n slipped inside, the warehouse's dimly lit interior stretching out before them. Stacks of shipping containers formed a labyrinth of potential cover, and the air was thick with the smell of oil and saltwater.

"Stay sharp," Zeke murmured.

The Confrontation

In the center of the warehouse, Diego stood with a briefcase in hand, flanked by two burly bodyguards. His nerves were evident in the way he shifted his weight from one foot to the other.

"Is this what you wanted?" Diego asked, opening the briefcase to reveal stacks of cash and a small black USB drive.

The man across from him—a shadowy figure in a tailored suit—nodded, reaching for the case.

Before the exchange could happen, Zeke stepped into the light, his voice cutting through the tension.

"Diego," he called out, his tone calm but commanding.

Diego froze, his eyes widening in shock. "Zeke? What the hell are you doing here?"

"Cleaning up your mess," Zeke replied, his gaze locked on the briefcase. "Hand it over."

The bodyguards moved to intercept, but Just'n was faster, taking them down with swift, precise strikes. The shadowy figure tried to flee, but Yasmeen's tranquilizer dart found its mark, dropping him instantly.

Diego, now cornered, looked at Zeke with a mix of fear and desperation. "You don't understand—"

"I understand more than you think," Zeke interrupted, stepping closer. "Now, give me the drive."

Reluctantly, Diego handed it over, his hands trembling.

"This isn't over," Diego warned, but Zeke was already walking away.

The Aftermath

Back at the villa, the team gathered around Yasmeen's computer as she decrypted the USB drive. The data revealed a network of offshore accounts and shipments linked to Henderson's operation.

"This is it," Yasmeen said, her green eyes gleaming with triumph. "This is the leverage we need."

Zeke leaned back in his chair, a small smile playing on his lips. "One step closer," he murmured, thinking of Autumn.

"Miami never disappoints," Just'n joked, raising a glass of champagne.

"Let's hope Portland is just as eventful," Yasmeen added, already planning their next move.

The team clinked their glasses together, but Zeke's mind was elsewhere. The scent of Autumn still lingered in his memory, driving him forward.

Hold on, Autumn, he thought. *I'm coming.*

"I am the creator of my reality. I attract limitless opportunities, abundance, and success. Nothing can stop me from achieving my highest potential."
—Paris D.

Chapter 24
NEXT MOVES IN MOTION

The Miami villa hummed with subdued energy as the team regrouped. The evidence from the USB drive was groundbreaking, a web of offshore accounts and shipments connecting Mr. Henderson's operations to larger international players. The villa felt like the calm before the storm—a brief moment to catch their breath before their next mission.

Zeke stood by the window, staring out at the sparkling Atlantic. His bronze dreadlocks were still damp from a quick shower, and the white tank top he wore revealed the tension rippling through his frame. The scent of the ocean air calmed him, but only slightly. He was too deep in thought.

"We need to move quickly," Yasmeen said, her voice cutting through the room. She was seated at the dining table, effortlessly elegant in a silk blouse and tailored slacks. A glass of red wine sat untouched in front of her. Her green eyes were sharp as ever, locked on the map sprawled out before her.

"Dream and Brandon are off the grid," Yasmeen added, glancing at Zeke. "They've relocated to Dubai for now. It's a good move—Henderson won't think to look for them there."

"Smart," Just'n said, leaning against the kitchen counter. His casual demeanor didn't hide the fire in his hazel eyes. "They need to lay low. This game is bigger than they realize."

Zeke nodded, but his focus remained on the horizon. "Good. They deserve some peace."

Akemi Returns to the Fold

The sound of heels clicking on the marble floor announced Akemi's arrival. She walked into the room like a storm contained in a human body. Her curly hair framed her glowing face, her golden-brown skin radiant under the villa's soft lighting. She wore a flowing coral maxi dress, its vibrant color mirroring her fiery energy.

"I hope I'm not interrupting," Akemi said, her tone sharp but not unkind.

"Always the dramatic entrance," Yasmeen quipped, smirking.

Akemi gave her a pointed look before turning her attention to Zeke. "We need to talk."

Zeke's eyes met hers, and he gave a slow nod. "Let's step outside."

The two walked out to the terrace, where the ocean breeze carried the scent of salt and jasmine. Akemi leaned against the railing, her expression unreadable.

"I've been keeping tabs on Diego," she said, cutting straight to the point. "I know you don't trust him—and you shouldn't—but he's still useful. For now."

Zeke's jaw tightened. "He's playing his own game. But that doesn't mean I can't use him to win mine."

Akemi tilted her head, a faint smile playing on her lips. "Always the strategist. Just be careful, Zeke. Diego's not as dumb as he looks."

Zeke's gaze softened slightly. "I know. But I also know you wouldn't let anything happen to me."

Akemi chuckled, shaking her head. "Don't get too comfortable. You might be my favorite, but that doesn't mean I'll save your ass every time."

The two shared a brief laugh, but the tension lingered. They both knew the stakes were too high for comfort.

Preparing For Portland

Back inside, Yasmeen was coordinating the logistics for their next mission. Portland was their next stop, and the evidence from the Miami operation had pointed to a major Henderson shipment set to dock there within days.

"We'll take the jet," Yasmeen said, her tone brisk as she tapped away on her tablet. "Akemi, I need you to tap into your Miami contacts before we leave. Zeke, you'll take point on the ground team again. Just'n, you're with me on recon."

"And what about Diego?" Just'n asked, raising an eyebrow.

"He's bait," Yasmeen said simply.

The room fell silent for a moment before Just'n let out a low whistle. "Cold as ever."

"It's not personal," Yasmeen replied, shrugging. "It's strategy."

As the night deepened, the team prepared to leave for Portland. The villa buzzed with quiet activity as bags were packed, weapons were checked, and plans were finalized.

Zeke found a moment alone on the terrace, the cool night air washing over him. He closed his eyes, trying to focus on the task ahead, but his thoughts kept drifting to Autumn.

"I'm coming for you," he whispered to the night.

Behind him, Yasmeen watched silently, her sharp green eyes filled with a rare softness. She respected Zeke's focus, his drive—but she also knew the burden he carried.

"Let's get this done," she said, stepping onto the terrace.

Zeke turned to her, a faint smile on his lips. "Yeah. Let's."

The two stood there for a moment, the sound of the ocean filling the silence, before heading back inside. The next phase of their mission awaited, and they were ready to face whatever came their way.

Chapter 25

PORTLAND PURSUIT

The jet descended smoothly through Portland's overcast sky, the city's famous rainy weather misting the windows. Yasmeen glanced up from her tablet as the plane touched down. Her green eyes, sharp and calculating, scanned the faces of her team. Everyone was quiet, focused. This mission would require precision.

The evidence they retrieved in Miami had pointed to this port as a hub for Henderson's illicit operations. A major shipment was scheduled to arrive tonight, one carrying contraband that tied directly to his empire—and potentially to Autumn.

Zeke adjusted his leather jacket as he stood. His bronze dreadlocks framed his face, and his hazel-green eyes burned with determination. He was ready for whatever came next.

"Game faces on," Yasmeen said as the group prepared to disembark. "Portland's not Miami. It's colder, wetter, and full of shadows. Keep your guard up."

Setting The Stage

The rain was steady as they stepped off the jet. Yasmeen had arranged for luxury SUVs to be waiting for them, their dark, sleek frames blending seamlessly with the night. The city's industrial port loomed

197

in the distance, its cranes silhouetted against the gray sky.

"Split up," Yasmeen instructed once they were in the cars. "Zeke, Akemi, and Just'n—head to the docks. That's where the shipment is landing. I'll set up the tech hub at the safe house and provide overwatch. Stay in constant contact."

"Got it," Zeke said, his voice low but resolute.

Akemi, sitting beside him in the back seat, crossed her arms. She was dressed in an all-black tactical outfit that hugged her frame, her curly hair tied back. Her golden-brown skin glowed faintly in the dim light of the car. She glanced at Zeke.

"You better not get us killed," she said, half-joking.

Zeke smirked. "Only if you don't slow me down."

Akemi rolled her eyes but couldn't hide the small smile tugging at her lips.

The Docks

The docks were a maze of shipping containers and towering cranes, their shadows stretching long in the dim light. The rain made the ground slick, and the air was heavy with the scent of salt and oil.

Zeke led the way, his movements quiet and deliberate. He'd dressed for stealth: a fitted black jacket, cargo pants, and combat boots. He'd always had a way of blending into the background, a skill honed from years of evading danger.

"Keep an eye out," he whispered to Akemi and Just'n, who flanked him on either side.

Just'n, towering at 6'3", moved with surprising grace for his size. His curly black hair was damp from the rain, and his hazel eyes scanned the area with precision. He held a silenced pistol, ready for anything.

Akemi carried a blade strapped to her thigh, her hand resting on its hilt. She didn't trust guns—they were too loud, too impersonal.

"Movement ahead," Just'n said, his voice barely audible through their earpieces.

Zeke followed his gaze. A group of men in dark clothing was unloading crates from a shipping container. Each crate was marked with a strange insignia—a goat's head.

"That's it," Zeke muttered.

Infiltration

The team moved closer, sticking to the shadows. Zeke could feel the tension in the air, the way his senses heightened as they approached.

"Hold position," Yasmeen's voice came through their earpieces. She was monitoring the scene from the safe house, her tech setup giving her a bird's-eye view of the docks. "There's a lot of heat in that area. At least ten guards armed to the teeth."

"Great," Akemi whispered. "Just what we needed."

"We're not here to fight," Zeke said. "We're here to gather intel and get out. Quietly."

The team crept closer, using the towering shipping containers as cover. Zeke's heart pounded as they reached the edge of the activity. He could hear the men talking, their voices gruff and tense.

One of them opened a crate, revealing an assortment of weapons and what looked like vials of an unidentified liquid.

"Bioweapons," Just'n muttered.

Zeke clenched his jaw. This was bigger than he'd thought.

A Close Call

As they moved to get a better vantage point, one of the guards turned suddenly, his flashlight sweeping the area.

"Down," Zeke hissed, and the team dropped to the ground, pressing themselves against the wet concrete.

The guard's light passed over them, lingering for a moment before moving on.

"That was too close," Akemi whispered, her breath visible in the cold night air.

Zeke didn't respond. He was focused on the crate the guard had opened. Something about it felt … familiar.

The Twist

Whle they prepared to retreat, Zeke noticed something inside one of the crates—a small, stuffed animal. It was a lamb, its white fur stained with dirt.

Zeke's heart stopped. He recognized it. It belonged to Autumn.

"She's here," he whispered, his voice trembling with a mix of hope and rage.

"What?" Akemi asked, her eyes wide.

"She's here," Zeke repeated, his fists clenching.

Escape

Before Zeke could act, Yasmeen's voice cut through their earpieces.

"Guys, you've got company. Three guards heading your way. Get out of there. Now."

Reluctantly, Zeke signaled for the team to fall back. They moved quickly but carefully, retracing their steps through the maze of containers.

As they reached the perimeter, a loud noise echoed through the docks—a gunshot.

"Go, go!" Zeke urged, and the team broke into a run.

They reached the SUV and piled in, Just'n taking the wheel. The tires screeched as they sped away from the scene, the rain pounding against the windows.

Back at the safe house, Yasmeen was waiting for them, her green eyes filled with concern.

"What happened?" she asked as they entered.

Zeke didn't answer immediately. He walked to the table, placed the stuffed lamb on it, and stared at it.

"She's alive," he said finally, his voice filled with conviction. "And we're going to get her back."

The room fell silent, the weight of his words sinking in.

Yasmeen stepped closer, placing a hand on his shoulder. "We will," she said firmly.

Outside, the rain continued to fall, but inside the safe house, the team's resolve burned brighter than ever.

Chapter 26

PORTLAND PURSUIT

Amy Lyons moved through the rain-soaked streets of Portland, her sharp eyes scanning the industrial port. The air here carried a weight she couldn't ignore—the faint, acrid tang of oil mingled with the metallic scent of danger. Her senses, always tuned to subtle environmental shifts, were on high alert.

She adjusted the strap of her eco-friendly leather satchel, which held her essential gadgets. Inside was her portable forensics scanner, a lightweight drone, and a customized tablet loaded with surveillance tools. She'd worked tirelessly to perfect her technology, combining her detective expertise with her passion for protecting the planet.

The call about the goat-head-masked network had come just days earlier. The dead hit-man found in Atlanta was tied to this shipment, and Amy's instincts told her there was more to uncover here than just weapons.

A Lone Investigator

Standing by her rented electric car—a sleek black Polestar 3—Amy glanced at her tablet. A thermal drone she'd launched earlier hovered over the docks, mapping heat signatures. She spotted clusters of guards and crates, their outlines vivid against the cool background.

"Got you," she murmured, zooming in on the live feed.

Her pale fingers tapped the screen, overlaying timestamps and noting movement patterns. She noticed a commotion near one of the containers—a group of guards scattering after a gunshot rang out.

Amy frowned. "What the hell's going on down there?"

Parallel Missions

Unbeknownst to her, Zeke and his team were making their escape just a few hundred yards away. Amy's drone briefly caught their fleeing SUV, but her focus was on the crate being reopened by a panicked guard.

She whispered into her voice recorder, her Irish lilt soft but determined. "Crate 47—priority target. Appears to contain liquid bioweapons. Need verification."

The rain intensified, drumming against the hood of her eco-friendly jacket. Amy adjusted her hood, her fiery red hair tucked neatly beneath it. She moved closer to the action, blending into the shadows.

As she reached the edge of the dock, the sound of waves crashing against the pilings reached her ears. She paused, her heightened awareness kicking in. Something wasn't right. The air felt … charged, almost electric.

Amy closed her eyes briefly, letting her senses guide her. The smell of saltwater mingled with something chemical. The distant caw of a seagull was abruptly silenced. She opened her eyes, now more focused than ever.

A Clue in the Rain

Amy crouched behind a stack of barrels, pulling out her portable scanner. She aimed it at the crate the guards had opened and detected faint traces of a sedative compound. Her jaw tightened. This wasn't just a weapons shipment—it was something far darker.

"Trafficking bioweapons under the guise of shipping materials," she muttered. "Classic Henderson."

Her earpiece crackled. It was her contact in Portland, a local environmentalist who had been feeding her intel on suspicious activities near the port.

"Amy, we've got a lead on another shipment. This one's heading to Seattle."

"Seattle?" Amy replied, her voice low. "I'm not done here yet."

"There's more," her contact said. "We think the same network might be tied to missing persons cases in the area. People disappearing near the coastline."

Amy's stomach turned. "Understood. Keep me updated."

A Narrow Escape

The guards were on high alert now, their voices sharp and urgent. Amy knew she needed to leave before she was spotted. She packed up her gear quickly, her movements precise and silent.

As she retreated to her car, she spotted something on the ground—a small stuffed lamb, damp from the rain. She picked it up, her fingers brushing against its worn fur.

"Why would this be here?" she whispered, her mind racing.

The sound of approaching footsteps pulled her from her thoughts. She slipped the lamb into her bag and hurried to her car, her heart pounding.

A New Piece of the Puzzle

Back at her hotel, Amy spread her findings across the desk. Photos, thermal images, and chemical analyses painted a grim picture. But the lamb nagged at her. It didn't fit with the rest of the evidence, and yet, it felt important.

As she sipped her herbal tea, she stared at the stuffed toy, her mind spinning with possibilities.

"Who are you connected to?" she murmured.

Amy didn't know it yet, but the lamb had already connected her investigation to Zeke's mission.

Foreshadowing

In another part of Portland, Zeke stared at the same type of lamb on the table in the safe house. His fists were clenched, his mind racing.

"She's alive," he said again, his voice firm.

Yasmeen leaned against the wall, watching him carefully. "Then we'd better move fast."

Neither Zeke nor Amy knew how close their paths were to crossing, but both felt the weight of their missions growing heavier by the second.

Amy's Next Steps

Amy leaned back in her chair, the weight of her discoveries pressing heavily on her. The stuffed lamb sat on the desk, its button eyes staring blankly ahead. She had seen countless clues in her career, but something about this one unsettled her in a way she couldn't explain.

After documenting her findings, she packed up her gear into her eco-friendly leather backpack. She double-checked her gadgets— drone, portable scanner, encrypted tablet—ensuring she was ready for whatever came next. The message from her Portland contact lingered in her mind. Missing persons. Bioweapons. Disappearances near the coast.

Amy stood by the window of her modest hotel room, overlooking the rain-soaked streets of Portland. The faint glow of neon lights reflected on the wet pavement. Her instincts screamed that she was close to uncovering something massive, but the complexity of it all made her head spin.

Her phone buzzed, jolting her from her thoughts. She answered, her Irish accent crisp. "Lyons here."

"Amy, you need to see this," her Portland contact said, their voice urgent.

"What is it?"

"We recovered footage from a dock camera before it was wiped. It shows the crate you flagged being moved onto a private yacht. The yacht's owner ... it's Henderson Corp."

Amy's stomach twisted. She had suspected Mr. Henderson's involvement, but now, she had proof.

"Send me the footage," she said, her voice firm. "And keep an eye on any departures. If that yacht moves, I want to know."

As soon as the footage arrived, Amy loaded it onto her tablet. The grainy video showed men in goat head masks unloading crates onto a sleek black yacht. The sight made her blood run cold.

"It's worse than I thought," she whispered.

Grabbing her keys, Amy headed for the docks. She wasn't going to let that yacht disappear without leaving her mark.

Zeke and his Team's Preparations

Meanwhile, in a hidden safe house on the outskirts of Portland, Zeke stood over a table covered with maps, photographs, and a scattering of weapons. His bronze dreadlocks were tied back, but a few strands framed his determined face. His hazel-green eyes glowed with intensity as he studied the layout of their next target—a mansion on the outskirts of Miami, rumored to be Henderson's fallback hideout.

Yasmeen paced nearby, her radiant black hair flowing as she moved with restless energy. She exuded confidence, her sharp green eyes never leaving Zeke.

"We need to hit Miami, Florida, fast," Zeke said, his voice low but commanding.

Yasmeen crossed her arms, her lips curving into a sly smile. "We'll hit it, but not recklessly. You've got me now, remember? Resources are my specialty."

Zeke glanced at her. He respected her brilliance, but he couldn't afford distractions. Especially not when Autumn's life was at stake.

Diego entered the room, his tone casual but his eyes guarded. "You keep talking about moving fast, but are you even sure Miami is where you need to be?"

Zeke's jaw tightened. He didn't trust Diego, not fully. The man had too many secrets, too much arrogance. But for now, he was a necessary ally.

"I'm sure," Zeke said. "And if you're not, stay out of my way."

Diego smirked, leaning back against the wall. "Relax, man. I'm just saying … you might want to make sure this isn't another trap."

Yasmeen stepped between them, her gaze icy. "Enough. We're not wasting time on bickering. Zeke knows what he's doing. If you're not on board, Diego, feel free to walk out that door."

Diego chuckled, raising his hands in mock surrender. "All right, all right. No need to get defensive."

A Strategic Shift

As the tension in the room simmered, Zeke reached into his pocket and pulled out a small, worn photograph of Autumn. His heart ached as he stared at her image, but it also strengthened his resolve.

"She's in Miami," Zeke said quietly. "I can feel it."

Yasmeen watched him, her expression softening for a brief moment. She respected Zeke's determination, even if it worried her.

"All the more reason to stay sharp," she said. "I've already got a team prepping our gear. We'll have everything we need when we get there."

Zeke nodded, then looked at Diego. "You're in or you're out. Decide now."

Diego hesitated, then sighed. "I'm in. But don't think for a second I'm doing this for you."

"I wouldn't dream of it," Zeke replied, his voice laced with sarcasm.

Yasmeen smirked, breaking the tension with a dry remark. "Great. Now that we're all friends, let's get moving."

As they finalized their plans, the faint sound of rain against the windows filled the room. Zeke's mind was already on Miami, Florida, his thoughts consumed by Autumn and the mission ahead.

Intersecting Paths

While Zeke's team prepared for Miami, Amy stood at the edge of the dock, her sharp eyes scanning the yacht. The rain had stopped, leaving a stillness in the air that felt almost ominous. She didn't know it yet, but her investigation was about to intersect with Zeke's mission in ways neither of them could anticipate.

Amy's Dockside Pursuit

The rain-soaked dock was eerily quiet as Amy crouched behind a stack of shipping crates. The faint scent of saltwater mixed with the sharp tang of gasoline from the boats bobbing nearby. Her eco-friendly leather boots barely made a sound against the slick wood as she shifted her weight, her breath steady despite her racing heart.

The yacht sat docked about fifty yards away, its sleek black exterior gleaming under the dim lights. Through her binoculars, Amy could see two men in goat head masks standing guard, their postures tense. She recognized the crates on the deck—identical to the ones she'd seen in the footage.

Her encrypted earpiece crackled. "Lyons, we've got confirmation. Those crates match the ones tied to Henderson Corp. You sure you don't want backup?"

Amy pressed a finger to her earpiece. "Negative. Backup will scare them off. I need to see where they're taking this shipment."

"Understood. Be careful."

Amy smirked to herself. "Always am."

She adjusted the strap of her bag, ensuring her drone and scanning equipment were within reach. As she crept closer to the yacht, her heightened senses kicked in. She could feel the subtle shift in the air—an unusual chill that sent a shiver down her spine. The water lapping against the dock sounded off, almost … unnatural.

Amy paused, her intuition urging her to wait. A low rumble echoed from the yacht's engine, followed by the faint sound of voices. She pulled out her drone and launched it, controlling it from her tablet. The drone hovered silently, its camera zooming in on the men loading the crates.

Then, she saw him. A man in a tailored suit, his sharp features partially obscured by shadows. It was unmistakably Diego.

Amy's stomach clenched. She'd read his file—Henderson's nephew, ruthless and cunning. Whatever he was doing here, it couldn't be good.

She captured the footage and began to retreat, knowing she'd need to follow the yacht when it departed. But as she turned to leave, a creak from the dock betrayed her position. One of the masked guards turned, his hand moving to his weapon.

"Who's there?" he barked, his voice cutting through the silence.

Amy froze, her heart pounding. She needed to move fast.

Zeke's Miami Mission

The Miami sun blazed down on the oceanfront mansion as Zeke, Yasmeen, and Diego's team approached from the beach side. The salty breeze ruffled Zeke's dreadlocks, and his hazel-green eyes scanned the sprawling property with precision.

Yasmeen walked beside him, her radiant black hair tied into a sleek ponytail. She wore a white tailored jumpsuit paired with gold-accented combat boots, looking like a goddess ready for war. "I hope this is worth the effort," she said, her tone laced with sarcasm.

"It will be," Zeke replied, his voice calm but firm.

Diego trailed behind them, wearing an uncharacteristically casual outfit—linen pants and a loose button-up shirt. But his body language betraycd his unease.

The plan was simple but dangerous: Infiltrate the mansion, gather intel on Henderson's Miami operations, and locate any leads on Autumn's whereabouts.

Zeke tightened the straps on his tactical vest, his mind laser-focused. He could sense Autumn's presence, faint but unmistakable, pulling at him like a thread.

As they neared the mansion, Yasmeen handed Zeke a small device. "Signal jammer," she explained. "It'll cut their comms for five minutes. Use it wisely."

Zeke gave her a rare smile. "You're always two steps ahead."

"I try," she replied, smirking.

Intersecting Paths

Back in Portland, Amy made her move. As the guard approached her position, she threw a small noise emitter to the opposite side of the dock. The device let out a high-pitched whine, drawing the guard's attention.

Amy slipped away, her heart pounding as she ducked behind a shipping container. She watched as the yacht's engines roared to life, the vessel pulling away from the dock.

Her earpiece crackled again. "Lyons, the yacht's heading south. We're tracking it. Destination appears to be … Miami."

Amy frowned. First Portland, now Miami? The pieces of the puzzle were falling into place, but the picture they formed was darker than she'd imagined.

As the yacht disappeared into the distance, Amy whispered to herself, "Whatever's waiting in Miami, I'm going to find out."

Closing the Loop

In Miami, Zeke's team breached the mansion with surgical precision. Yasmeen's resources ensured their entry was flawless, but the tension in the air was palpable.

Zeke moved through the lavish halls like a shadow, his mind racing with thoughts of Autumn. Diego played his part, but Zeke kept a close eye on him, knowing the man couldn't be trusted.

They reached a secured room filled with files and surveillance equipment. Yasmeen worked quickly, her fingers flying over the keyboard of a stolen laptop.

"Got something," she said, her green eyes gleaming. "Coordinates … and a list of shipments. One's headed to Portland."

Zeke's jaw tightened. *Portland again?* The web was growing more complex by the second.

As they extracted the data, Zeke felt a strange pull, like the world was nudging him toward something important.

In Portland, Amy stood at her hotel room window, staring out at the city. Her investigation was leading her to Miami, to the same chaos Zeke was diving headfirst into.

Though their paths hadn't crossed yet, destiny was weaving their stories together.

Chapter 27

CONVERGING PATHS

Amy Lyons in Portland

The fog hung low over Portland's steel bridges as Amy Lyons stepped out of the eco-friendly cab, her boots crunching softly on the gravel near the dock. Her heightened awareness kicked in immediately; the air carried a faint metallic scent that felt out of place. The seagulls overhead were unusually quiet, and the water lapping against the pier seemed unnaturally still. Something was wrong here.

Amy adjusted the strap of her canvas satchel, stuffed with gadgets of her own design: a portable spectrometer, a handheld salinity scanner, and a thermal imaging camera. Each tool had helped her unravel countless environmental mysteries, but this case was far more sinister. The goat head mask found in Portland had a clear connection to the ocean, and she was determined to find the threads that tied it all together.

Her phone buzzed. She glanced at it, expecting another call from her father, but instead, it was an encrypted message from one of her marine conservation contacts. It was a photo of another goat head mask, found washed ashore on the Oregon coast. Beneath it, the message read: *This isn't just local. They're everywhere.*

Amy's jaw tightened. She made a mental note to investigate further, but first, she had to follow up on the warehouse lead. As she moved toward the dockside warehouse, she noted the eerie silence of her surroundings. The stillness was only interrupted by the occasional groan of the structure under its own weight.

The door creaked open as she stepped inside, greeted by the faint scent of salt and something metallic—blood. Her sharp eyes scanned the space, noticing faint drag marks on the dusty floor leading to the corner of the room. Kneeling, she pulled out her thermal camera. As the image resolved, she saw what appeared to be a faint handprint glowing in residual heat. Someone had been here recently.

Zeke's Portland Mission

Elsewhere in Portland, Zeke stood on the rooftop of a dilapidated high-rise, the wind tugging at his bronze dreads. His hazel-green eyes scanned the skyline, reflecting the fiery sunset. Yasmeen stood beside him, her long black hair billowing like a goddess in the golden light. She wore a sleek leather jacket and tailored combat pants, her green eyes sharp and alert.

"We move in thirty minutes," Zeke said, his voice calm but carrying an edge of urgency.

"Are we sure Diego can pull his weight?" Yasmeen asked, her tone laced with doubt.

Zeke smirked, but there was no humor in it. "He's not pulling weight— he's being pulled. Let him think he's running the show."

Yasmeen chuckled softly, but her expression sobered as she glanced at him. "You've got a lot riding on this. Autumn's alive—I can feel it, but we can't afford to lose focus."

Zeke nodded, his mind flickering back to the faint scent of Autumn he'd picked up on Diego during their last encounter. The memory fueled his determination. "We'll get her back, Yas. I'll tear this whole operation apart if I have to."

As they prepared for their mission, the team loaded up in their luxury SUV—a bulletproof, matte-black Range Rover equipped with state-of-the-art tech. Yasmeen, ever the resourceful one, handed Zeke a pair of augmented reality glasses she'd designed herself.

"Consider these a gift," she said, smirking. "Real-time mapping, thermal vision, and comms. You're welcome."

Zeke slid them on, the interface springing to life. "Nice. Remind me to never underestimate your genius."

Crossing Paths Without Knowing

Unbeknownst to either party, Amy's investigation and Zeke's mission were converging. The warehouse Amy had entered was the same one Zeke and his team had set their sights on for intel extraction. While Amy uncovered more evidence, the faint sound of vehicles approaching from outside reached her ears. She instinctively hid in the shadows, watching as Yasmeen, Zeke, and Diego entered with precision.

Amy's breath caught as she observed the group. They moved like a well-oiled machine, but there was something raw about the man with the bronze dreads—an energy she couldn't quite place. She stayed hidden, knowing her presence could compromise everything.

As Zeke and his team moved deeper into the warehouse, Amy slipped out quietly, her mind racing. Whoever they were, they weren't ordinary criminals. And something told her their mission was tied to the masks, the ocean, and possibly even the larger threat she was chasing.

While she disappeared into the foggy night, Zeke paused, his senses tingling. "Did you hear that?" he asked, his hazel-green eyes narrowing.

Yasmeen glanced around. "Nothing but the wind, Zeke. Let's keep moving."

But Zeke wasn't convinced. Something—or someone—had been there.

Amy sat in her eco-friendly rental car, staring out at the water as rain began to fall. Her gut told her she was getting closer to the truth, but the pieces of the puzzle still didn't fit. Meanwhile, Zeke and his team stood over the documents they'd retrieved, their expressions grim as they unraveled yet another layer of Mr. Henderson's sinister web.

Two paths, destined to collide, were inching closer with every passing moment. Neither Amy nor Zeke knew it yet, but their fates were intertwined in a way that would change everything.

Chapter 28

Wrapping Up the Portland, Oregon, Mission

The cool, damp air of Portland clung to the team as they moved silently through the shadows of the old industrial complex. The goat-head-masked figures they had been tracking had vanished into the night, but their mission wasn't a complete failure. Among the discarded crates and rusted machinery, Zeke uncovered a coded map embedded in the back of a leather-bound journal. The symbols pointed toward Miami, Florida, tying everything back to the chaos unfolding there.

Yasmeen's sharp green eyes flicked over the map, her expression unreadable. She seemed almost distracted, her usual intensity subdued. She leaned closer to Zeke, speaking low enough that only he could hear.

"This is bigger than we thought," she murmured, tracing the edge of the map with her manicured fingers. "But Miami isn't my next stop."

Zeke glanced at her sharply. "What do you mean?"

Yasmeen straightened, her radiant figure illuminated by a sliver of moonlight streaming through the broken windows. "I have my own loose ends to tie up. Miami's a distraction for me now."

"You're chasing her, aren't you?" Zeke asked, his voice steady but heavy with implication. He didn't have to say the name.

Yasmeen gave a small, knowing smile. "Miami isn't the only one running." She tucked the journal into his hand. "You can handle this. I've got bigger prey."

Just'n approached, his towering frame and sunlit presence radiating calm in the tension. "We need to move," he said, his voice firm. "The jet's fueled and waiting, and we've already pushed our luck staying here."

Dream's voice crackled over their comms. "Get out of there now. Local law enforcement is sweeping the area, and I'm not bailing anyone out of jail tonight."

The team nodded in unison, the mission in Portland finally coming to a close. As they exited the building, Zeke lagged behind, his mind swirling with Yasmeen's cryptic departure and the way her green eyes lingered on him just a second too long.

Yasmeen's Hunt

The private jet cut through the frigid air, heading east toward Russia. Yasmeen sat alone in the luxurious cabin, her thoughts far from the Portland mission and her team. She toyed with the ring she wore—a simple silver band with intricate engravings that no one knew the meaning of.

The real hunt was beginning. Miami, the elusive assassin who had once been her closest ally, was somewhere in Russia, and Yasmeen had vowed to find her. Their last encounter had ended in betrayal, blood, and unresolved questions. Yasmeen's resources were unparalleled— her wealth, her connections, her skill—but she knew Miami wouldn't be easy to corner.

As the plane began its descent, she stared out the window at the sprawling Russian wilderness. Snow blanketed the trees below, a pristine canvas hiding the danger that lay ahead. Yasmeen's lips curved into a sly smile.

"Time to finish this," she whispered.

Back in Portland, the team prepared to head to Miami, unaware of the storm brewing across the world.

"With a heart so pure I am a multimillionaire!"
—Paris D.

Chapter 29
THE MIAMI MISSION RESUMES

The sun blazed high over the Miami skyline, reflecting off the sleek black SUVs that carried the team through the bustling streets. The heat was relentless, wrapping around them like a smothering blanket. Palm trees lined the boulevards, swaying lazily in the humid breeze, while luxury yachts dotted the turquoise waters of Biscayne Bay. Miami was alive with its usual vibrancy, but beneath the glitz, danger simmered.

Zeke sat in the passenger seat, his long bronze dreadlocks tied back to keep the humidity at bay. He adjusted his black linen shirt, the fabric clinging to his caramel skin, and scanned the streets for anything suspicious. Though outwardly calm, his hazel-green eyes burned with determination. Autumn was still in the hands of Mr. Henderson, and every second felt like an eternity.

Just'n, sitting behind the wheel, glanced at Zeke, breaking the silence. "You good? You've been staring out that window for ten minutes straight."

Zeke's lips twitched into a faint smile. "Just thinking. Miami feels … different."

"Different how?" Just'n asked, his tone light but his curiosity genuine.

"Like the air's holding its breath. Something's about to break," Zeke replied, his voice low.

Dream's voice came through their earpieces, clear and commanding. "Focus, boys. We're not here to soak up the sun. The intel points to Henderson's nephew, Diego, operating out of a private club in South Beach. He's hosting a 'business' meeting tonight, and you need to get in there."

"Got it," Zeke said, his jaw tightening.

The Club Infiltration

Night fell, and the city came alive with neon lights and pulsating beats. Zeke and Just'n stepped out of their SUV, blending seamlessly with the glamorous crowd outside the exclusive club. Zeke had swapped his casual outfit for a tailored white Dolce & Gabbana suit that contrasted sharply against his bronze skin, while Just'n opted for a sleek black Kiton Suit ensemble that complemented his striking hazel eyes.

As they approached the velvet ropes, Just'n handed over a forged invitation, his confidence unshakable. The bouncer barely glanced at it before stepping aside.

Inside, the club was a sensory overload. Crystal chandeliers hung above a massive dance floor packed with Miami's elite. The scent of expensive perfume mingled with the faint aroma of cigars, and the thumping bass of the music vibrated through the floor.

Zeke scanned the room, his eyes locking onto Diego, who stood in a private VIP section surrounded by security. His slim, toned figure was draped in a Gucci designer suit, his light skin glowing under the dim lights. He looked calm, but Zeke could sense the tension in his body language.

"Target acquired," Zeke muttered into the comms.

"Remember," Dream's voice warned, "Diego's slippery. Don't let your guard down for a second."

The Confrontation

Zeke and Just'n made their way to the VIP area, their movements smooth and calculated. As they approached, Diego's gaze flicked to them, a small smirk playing on his lips.

"Zeke," Diego said, raising his glass. "I didn't expect to see you here. Finally taking a break from saving the world?"

Zeke smiled coolly. "Something like that. Thought I'd check in on an old friend."

Diego's eyes narrowed slightly, but he maintained his composure. "Friend, huh? Funny. I don't remember us being that close."

Just'n stepped forward, his towering presence intimidating the security guards nearby. "We're not here to reminisce, Diego. We need answers."

Diego leaned back in his chair, feigning nonchalance. "Answers about what?"

"You know exactly what," Zeke said, his voice dangerously low. "Autumn. Where is she?"

Diego's smirk faltered for a split second before he recovered. "I have no idea what you're talking about."

Zeke's eyes darkened, and for a moment, the air around him seemed to shift. Objects on the table trembled slightly, unnoticed by anyone but Diego.

Diego's face paled. "Relax, Zeke. You don't want to cause a scene here."

"Then start talking," Zeke demanded, leaning in close.

Back at the Safe House

Hours later, the team regrouped at their Miami safe house, a sleek beachfront property hidden behind high walls and lush greenery. The confrontation with Diego had been intense, but they had managed to extract crucial information: a lead on one of Mr. Henderson's operations in the Florida Keys.

Dream paced the living room, her sharp eyes darting between Zeke and Just'n. "We've got our next move. But this is going to be dangerous. Henderson's men will be waiting for us."

Zeke nodded, his mind already focused on the mission ahead. He glanced out at the moonlit ocean, the waves crashing gently against the shore. Somewhere out there, Autumn was waiting for him, and he would stop at nothing to bring her home.

Flashback:
The Bond Forged in Chaos

It was five years ago, deep in the sprawling chaos of Dubai's desert outskirts, when the three first crossed paths. The mission had been a high-stakes extraction, orchestrated by an underground network that specialized in cleaning up messes the world wasn't supposed to know about. Zeke, Yasmeen, and Just'n had all been hired separately, unaware they were about to form a bond that would change their lives forever.

The Setup

The target was a rogue arms dealer, Viktor Radevic, hiding in an abandoned luxury resort—a monument to excess, now swallowed by the relentless desert sands. The heat was suffocating, and the air shimmered under the relentless sun. The resort's shattered windows reflected shards of light as armed guards patrolled its perimeter.

Zeke had been the rookie back then, barely twenty-two, with his bronze dreadlocks tied back and his youthful determination blazing in his hazel-green eyes. His role was reconnaissance—a natural fit for someone with a sharp mind and subtle psychic abilities he didn't fully understand yet.

Just'n, the seasoned operative, was the leader of his own small team at the time. At twenty-eight, his towering 6'3" frame and radiant presence commanded respect. With his curly black hair and hazel eyes, he was the calm anchor in the storm. His job was to neutralize threats swiftly and cleanly.

And then there was Yasmeen, the wild card. At twenty-six, the stunning Russian millionaire with long black hair and piercing green eyes was both brilliant and deadly. Her beauty often disarmed people, but her precision with a sniper rifle and her resourcefulness made her a force to be reckoned with. She had been hired for long-range support, her perch atop the resort's crumbling rooftop giving her the perfect vantage point.

The Clash and the Connection

Their paths first collided when Zeke, still a little green, stumbled into Yasmeen's line of sight while scouting the perimeter. She could have taken him out in an instant, mistaking him for an enemy, but something about his youthful determination gave her pause.

"You're going to get yourself killed, мальчик (boy)," she said over the comms, her Russian accent sharp yet smooth.

Zeke, startled, froze in place. "Who the hell are you?"

"Your guardian angel, apparently," she replied dryly.

Just'n, listening in, chimed in from his own comm channel. "Enough chatter. We've got guards heading your way, Zeke. Keep moving."

From that moment, they were forced to coordinate, their survival dependent on their ability to trust one another.

The Ambush

Everything went sideways when Viktor's men discovered their infiltration. Bullets rained down as the team was pinned in the resort's crumbling banquet hall, the once-opulent space now a battlefield.

Zeke, armed with only a knife and a handgun, found himself cornered by two guards. His breathing was ragged, sweat dripping down his face as he tried to focus. Suddenly, the air around him seemed to shift, and in a moment of sheer desperation, the knife in his hand flew from his grip as if guided by an invisible force, embedding itself in one of the guard's necks.

The second guard hesitated, giving Zeke enough time to grab his gun and take him down. Yasmeen, watching from her rooftop perch, was the only one who noticed the strange way Zeke's movements had influenced the environment.

"I saw that," she murmured over the comms.

"Saw what?" Zeke replied, trying to catch his breath.

"Your secret," Yasmeen said cryptically, before firing a clean shot that took out another guard advancing on Just'n.

Just'n, meanwhile, had been covering their escape route, his every move calculated and precise. He fought with an efficiency that seemed almost choreographed, his hazel eyes scanning the chaos with laser focus. When the dust settled, it was Just'n who led the group to safety, his calm demeanor holding them together.

The Aftermath

They regrouped in an abandoned safe house just outside the city, the adrenaline still coursing through their veins. Yasmeen cleaned her sniper rifle with meticulous care, her green eyes flicking to Zeke every so often.

"You're more than you appear," she said finally, breaking the silence.

Zeke shrugged, trying to downplay what had happened. "I'm just good under pressure."

"Liar," Yasmeen said with a smirk, but she didn't press further.

Just'n leaned back in his chair, his usual calm laced with a hint of amusement. "I don't know how we pulled that off, but you two are something else."

From that day forward, the three became an inseparable team, each bringing something unique to the table. Zeke's resourcefulness and hidden abilities, Just'n's leadership and unshakable focus, and Yasmeen's unmatched precision and cunning made them a formidable trio.

Though their paths would eventually diverge, the bond they formed in Dubai remained unbreakable—a connection forged in fire and chaos.

Take a deep breath and let these words settle into your being. You are powerful, you are beautiful, and you are exactly where you need to be.
—Paris D.

Chapter 30

THE CALM BEFORE THE STORM

Back in Miami, the team had regrouped at an ultra-luxurious penthouse overlooking the ocean, a safe house provided by Just'n's extensive network. The sprawling suite was nothing short of extravagant, with floor-to-ceiling windows framing a view of the turquoise waters, sleek marble floors, and a private infinity pool on the terrace. Despite the serene setting, an air of tension hung thick among them as they prepared for the next phase of their mission.

The Team Regroups

Zeke leaned against the glass wall, the sunlight catching the bronze tones in his dreadlocks. His hazel-green eyes were sharp, focused on the distant horizon. Despite his calm exterior, his mind raced with thoughts of Autumn. Every moment they delayed felt like an eternity, and the fact that Yasmeen had left for Russia weighed heavily on him. She had always been their secret weapon, her resources and cunning a crucial advantage.

Dream and Brandon had checked in briefly, letting the group know they were lying low in Dubai, a temporary retreat funded by Yasmeen before her departure. That left Zeke, Just'n, Akemi, and Diego as the core team in Miami.

Diego, ever the enigma, sat on the leather sectional, his slim frame relaxed, but his light eyes gave away his unease. He twirled a silver lighter between his fingers, a nervous tic that irritated Akemi to no end.

"Can you not?" Akemi snapped, her voice sharp as she adjusted the strap of her sleeveless white jumpsuit. The outfit clung perfectly to her toned frame, exuding effortless elegance. "We're trying to focus." Diego smirked but pocketed the lighter. "Relax, Akemi. I'm not the one losing my cool."

"Yet," she shot back, her light eyes narrowing.

Just'n, ever the mediator, stepped between them, his 6'3" frame towering over the both of them. "All right, enough," he said firmly, his deep voice cutting through the tension. "We don't have time for this. We've got intel coming in soon, and we need to be ready."

Mission Briefing

The group gathered around the penthouse's sleek glass dining table, where Akemi had laid out a map of Miami alongside a series of encrypted files.

"Our contact says there's a shipment coming into the harbor tomorrow night," Akemi began, her tone all business. "It's tied to Mr. Henderson's operations—probably weapons or something bigger. If we can intercept it, we might get closer to finding Autumn."

Zeke clenched his jaw, his mind flashing to the memory of Autumn's laugh, her smile. He couldn't let himself imagine the worst.

"I'll take the harbor," Zeke said, his voice low but firm.

Just'n nodded. "Not alone, you won't. Diego, you're with him." Diego raised an eyebrow but didn't argue.

"What about me?" Akemi asked, crossing her arms.

"You'll stay here and coordinate," Just'n replied.

Akemi bristled but didn't push back. She knew Just'n's logic was sound—her strengths were in strategy and planning, not fieldwork.

Unforeseen Interruptions

While the team wrapped up their plans, Zeke's phone buzzed. He glanced at the screen, his heart skipping a beat. It was a text, an untraceable number.

You're close, but not close enough. Keep digging. — Y

His eyes widened. Yasmeen. Even from Russia, she was still watching, still pulling strings.

"What is it?" Just'n asked, noticing Zeke's expression.

"Nothing," Zeke said quickly, slipping the phone back into his pocket.

The Calm Before the Chaos

While night fell, the team scattered to prepare for the mission. Zeke stepped out onto the terrace, the ocean breeze brushing against his face. He closed his eyes, trying to clear his mind, but the weight of everything threatened to crush him.

Akemi joined him, her expression softer than it had been earlier.

"Hey," she said, leaning on the railing beside him.
"Hey," Zeke replied, not looking at her.

"You're going to find her," Akemi said quietly.

Zeke finally turned to her, his hazel-green eyes meeting hers. "I have to."

"And you will," she said firmly. Then, with a rare smile, she added, "But maybe don't get yourself killed in the process. You're not that easy to replace."

A small chuckle escaped Zeke's lips, the tension in his shoulders easing slightly.

"Thanks, Akemi," he said.

"Anytime," she replied, turning to head back inside.

Zeke stayed on the terrace a moment longer, staring out at the endless ocean. Tomorrow, the storm would come, but for now, there was still a fleeting moment of calm.

Chapter 31

THE HARBOR HEIST AND TERESA'S RECOVERY

The Miami night air was thick with humidity, carrying the faint scent of saltwater and the distant hum of traffic. Underneath the glitz and glamour of the city, Zeke and his team prepared for the harbor mission. But even as Zeke tried to focus, his thoughts kept drifting to Teresa, his older sister.

Teresa's Recovery

Back in Atlanta, Teresa was beginning to heal, though the scars of her torture were far from just physical. The brutal events at the old warehouse had left her with deep psychological wounds. The news was relentless, with every major network—WCKID News in particular—covering the story for months.

Footage of Teresa being carried out of the warehouse on a stretcher had gone viral, sparking national outrage. The image of her bruised and battered body, her clothes torn and her face streaked with dried blood, had become the face of the investigation into Mr. Henderson's criminal empire.

Now, seven months later, Teresa was living in a secured safe house provided by Just'n's network, with round-the-clock care. Her caramel complexion had regained some of its warmth, but her body was still weak, her movements slow.

As she sat on the couch, flipping through a news channel that was, yet again, covering her story, Teresa's hands trembled. The reporters speculated about the ongoing investigation, linking her ordeal to the infamous Mr. Henderson and his twisted network.

Her nurse, a kind older woman named Sheila, appeared with a tray of herbal tea.

"Turn that off," Sheila said gently, taking the remote from Teresa. "You don't need to be watching that garbage."

Teresa sighed, leaning back into the cushions. "It's not garbage if it's the truth, Sheila."

Sheila gave her a stern look. "You've come too far to let them drag you back there. Focus on healing, not headlines."

But Teresa's mind was elsewhere. She thought about Autumn, still missing. Guilt gnawed at her every day. She was recovering, but Autumn was still in Mr. Henderson's clutches—or worse.

Her phone buzzed on the coffee table. It was Zeke.

"Hey, little brother," she said, her voice soft but tinged with fatigue.

"Hey, T," Zeke replied, his voice a mixture of relief and tension. "How're you holding up?"

"I've been better," she admitted. "But I'm here. That's what matters, right?"

Zeke paused. "I'll find her, Teresa. I promise."

Teresa closed her eyes, tears slipping down her cheeks. "Just … be careful, Zeke. Don't do something stupid trying to save us all."

"I won't," Zeke said, though they both knew it was a lie.

The Harbor Mission Begins

Meanwhile, back in Miami, Florida, Zeke, Just'n, Akemi, and Diego were gathered in an unmarked van parked a block away from the harbor. The air inside was tense, the kind of quiet that only comes before chaos.

Akemi, dressed in sleek black tactical gear that hugged her petite frame, checked her weapons. Her curls were pulled back into a tight ponytail, and her light eyes scanned the area with precision.

Just'n, towering over everyone in his dark, tailored combat attire, leaned against the side of the van, his usually warm demeanor replaced with sharp focus.

Diego, his usual smugness subdued, was sharpening a blade, the metallic sound grating against everyone's nerves.

Zeke, in his own lightweight tactical outfit, checked the comms. His hazel-green eyes burned with determination.

"All right," Akemi said, breaking the silence. "The shipment is set to arrive at Dock 14 in twenty minutes. Security is tight, but we've got access codes, thanks to Yasmeen's intel before she left. Zeke, you and Diego are on retrieval. Just'n and I will cover from the perimeter."

"And if things go south?" Diego asked, his tone casual but his eyes sharp.

"Then we adapt," Just'n said firmly.

As they stepped out of the van, the warm Miami breeze hit them. The harbor was illuminated by the glow of massive floodlights, the water reflecting their light like liquid gold. The distant sound of waves lapping against the docks mixed with the low hum of engines from cargo ships.

Zeke felt a strange calm wash over him. He was in his element now, and nothing—not even Mr. Henderson—was going to stop him from getting one step closer to saving Autumn.

The Action Unfolds

The team moved like shadows, slipping through the maze of shipping containers and avoiding the armed guards patrolling the area.

Zeke and Diego reached the target container, its doors padlocked. Zeke pulled out a small device—a gift from Yasmeen before she left—that bypassed the lock with ease.

Inside, the shipment was nothing short of horrifying: crates filled with high-powered weapons, counterfeit money, and strange vials of an unknown substance.

"What the hell is this?" Diego whispered, his face pale.

"Evidence," Zeke said, snapping pictures with a small camera.

Suddenly, a shout rang out. They'd been spotted.

"Move!" Zeke barked, grabbing a crate and shoving it toward Diego.

The guards descended, bullets ricocheting off the metal containers. Just'n and Akemi provided cover fire, their precision keeping the attackers at bay.

Zeke's mind was laser-focused as he and Diego hauled the crate toward the extraction point. But even in the chaos, he couldn't shake the nagging feeling that this mission was just a piece of a much larger puzzle.

"Let go of doubt, let go of fear. You are already whole. Every step you take is leading you toward growth, toward wisdom, toward a deeper understanding of your own magic. Trust yourself. Honor yourself and spread love and light!"
—Paris D.

Chapter 32

SHADOWS OF THE PAST

The Miami harbor was silent now, safe from the faint echo of distant sirens as the team sped away in their getaway van. Zeke stared out of the window, his hazel-green eyes reflecting the city lights. The adrenaline from the mission still pulsed through his veins, but his mind was elsewhere—back in 2012, to a time when everything changed.

Flashback:
2012 — The First Meeting

Zeke was just nineteen, wide-eyed and hungry for something more than the mundane routine of his life in Atlanta. Autumn, barely a year older, was the fire to his calm—a fierce, vibrant woman with big dreams and a knack for charming her way into anything. They were inseparable, partners in everything, though Zeke always wondered if Autumn saw him as more than just her closest ally.

That summer, they found themselves at a high-stakes poker game in an underground club. Zeke had no business being there, but Autumn convinced him it was the perfect opportunity to test her skills.

"Trust me, Zeke," she whispered as they walked through the smoky, dimly lit room. "This is how we start making real money."

Zeke wasn't sure, but he followed her anyway.

At the center of the room sat Diego. He was twenty-four, already exuding the confidence of someone who had seen too much and survived it all. His slim build, sharp suit, and piercing gaze made him stand out. Women fluttered around him like moths to a flame, and the men, though wary, couldn't help but gravitate toward him.

Autumn's charm worked its magic, and before long, she and Zeke were sitting across the table from Diego.

"Who are these kids?" Diego asked with a smirk, his light skin glowing under the dim chandelier.

"Not kids," Autumn shot back, her radiant smile disarming. "We're opportunity waiting to happen."

Diego laughed, intrigued by her audacity. "Opportunity, huh? Show me."

By the end of the night, Autumn had managed to swindle her way to a small fortune. Zeke played the quiet observer, his mind racing as he pieced together Diego's moves.

After the game, Diego called them over.

"You've got potential," he said, lighting a cigar. "But potential's nothing without guidance. You want to survive this world? You need someone to teach you the rules. Lucky for you, I'm feeling generous."

From that day on, Diego took them under his wing. He taught them everything: how to run cons, how to navigate the underworld, and, most importantly, how to survive. But his mentorship came with a price.

Present Day: Driving Forward

Zeke snapped back to the present as Akemi nudged his arm.

"You've been quiet," she said, her voice low enough that only he could hear.

"Just thinking," Zeke replied, his tone guarded.

Akemi studied him, her light eyes narrowing. She didn't press further but gave him a look that said she'd be waiting when he was ready to talk.

In the front seat, Just'n drove with laser focus, while Diego sat beside him, scrolling through his phone.

"Good job out there tonight," Diego said casually, not bothering to look up.

Zeke fought the urge to smirk. Diego had no idea that he was already a pawn in Zeke's plan.

A Larger Game in Play

As the van sped through the Miami streets, Zeke's thoughts drifted to Autumn again. Diego had been the one to introduce them to this life, but he was also the one who might know where she was.

He closed his eyes, the memory of her laughter and the feel of her hand on his arm playing like a loop in his mind.

"Hold on, Autumn," Zeke muttered under his breath. "I'm coming for you."

To be continued …

Firestorm in Miami

The van had just turned onto a quiet stretch of road, the glow of the city dimming behind them, when the first shot shattered the silence.

CRACK!

The bullet tore through the back window, sending glass flying. Akemi ducked instinctively, her hand going to the pistol holstered at her side.

"Ambush!" Just'n shouted, slamming his foot on the gas. The van lurched forward, swerving as more bullets ricocheted off the metal frame.

Diego cursed, pulling a Glock from his waistband. "What the hell is this?" he barked, rolling down the window.

"They must've tracked us," Zeke muttered, his hazel-green eyes darting to the side mirror. Two black SUVs were closing in fast, their headlights cutting through the dark.

Zeke reached under the seat and pulled out a sleek shotgun, the weight of it familiar in his hands. "Akemi, stay low and cover me," he ordered, his voice calm but firm.

Akemi didn't hesitate. She rolled down her window, her sharp eyes narrowing as she aimed at the closest SUV.

BANG! BANG!

Her shots shattered the windshield of the pursuing vehicle, causing it to swerve violently.

"Nice shot," Zeke said with a smirk, pumping his shotgun. He leaned out of the van, aiming for the tires of the second SUV.

The roar of the shotgun echoed through the street as the slug found its mark. The SUV veered off the road, slamming into a parked car with a deafening crash.

"One down," Zeke muttered, pulling himself back into the van as Just'n took a sharp turn onto a side street.

But the first SUV was still on their tail, and now, another black sedan was joining the chase.

"This is getting ridiculous," Diego growled, leaning out of the passenger side window. He fired a volley of shots at the sedan, but it kept coming.

Suddenly, the van skidded to a stop.

"What are you doing?" Diego yelled, turning to Just'n.

"Switching tactics," Just'n replied, his hazel eyes blazing. He threw the van into reverse and slammed on the gas, ramming into the approaching SUV with a bone-rattling crunch.

The impact sent the SUV spinning, but the sedan skidded to a halt, and four masked men spilled out, guns drawn.

"Move!" Zeke shouted, kicking the van door open.

The group spilled out, weapons blazing. Zeke and Just'n moved with calculated precision, covering each other as they advanced. Akemi darted to the side, her movements fluid as she picked off one of the gunmen with a well-placed shot.

Diego, despite his frustration, fought with ruthless efficiency, his shots dropping two more attackers.

The last masked man hesitated, clearly realizing he was outmatched.

But before he could retreat, Yasmeen's voice crackled through Zeke's earpiece.

"Look up."

Zeke glanced up just in time to see Yasmeen's drone hovering above. A small device dropped from it, landing near the masked man's feet.

BOOM!

The explosion was controlled but powerful enough to knock the man off his feet.

"Mission assist complete," Yasmeen's voice purred over the comm. "You're welcome."

Zeke shook his head, a faint smile tugging at his lips. "Always the showoff," he muttered.

The team quickly regrouped, piling back into the van as sirens began to wail in the distance.

As they sped away, Zeke glanced at Diego. "Still think this is a game?"

Diego said nothing, but the look in his eyes spoke volumes.

Akemi leaned back in her seat, her adrenaline still pumping. "So … what's the plan now?"

Zeke's eyes glinted with determination. "We head back to base, regroup, and then we finish this. Miami's just the beginning."

Chapter 33
Unraveling the Maze

The safe house in Miami was quiet, nestled behind high, dense palms that shielded it from prying eyes. The team had returned from the chaotic streets, the air heavy with tension and adrenaline still coursing through their veins.

Zeke leaned against the kitchen counter, his bronze dreadlocks framing his face as he sipped a glass of water. His hazel-green eyes scanned the room, taking in the weight of their situation. They had won the skirmish, but it was clear the war was far from over.

"Yasmeen's drone saved our necks out there," Akemi said, tossing her gun on the table and collapsing onto the couch. "But why isn't she here? We could use her crazy resources right now."

"She's handling her own mission," Zeke said curtly, his tone leaving no room for further questions.

Diego sat across the room, his face a mix of exhaustion and irritation. He had been uncharacteristically quiet since the ambush, his sharp tongue subdued by whatever thoughts were eating at him.

"Diego," Zeke called, his voice calm but laced with authority. "Anything you want to tell us about that ambush?"

Diego's light-brown eyes flicked up to meet Zeke's, his jaw tightening.

"You think I set that up?"

"I think it's interesting how they seemed to know exactly where we were," Zeke replied, his tone even.

Akemi tensed, her gaze shifting between the two men. She didn't trust Diego, not after everything that had happened, but she didn't want to jump to conclusions.

"Enough," Just'n said, stepping into the room. His presence was commanding, his tall frame and sun-kissed skin radiating authority. "Pointing fingers isn't going to help us. We need to focus on the next move."

"And what's that?" Akemi asked, crossing her arms.

Just'n tossed a folder onto the table. "Intel from Yasmeen before she left. There's another location tied to Henderson's operations. A warehouse on the outskirts of Key Biscayne. It's heavily guarded, but if there's any clue about where Autumn is, it's there."

Zeke's hand tightened around his glass, the thought of Autumn strapped to a bed, drugged and helpless, fueling his resolve.

"We go tonight," Zeke said. "We've waited long enough."

Diego leaned back in his chair, a smug smirk creeping onto his face. "You're eager to walk into another trap, huh?"

Zeke's eyes narrowed. "You don't have to come. In fact, I'd prefer it."

"Enough!" Akemi snapped, rising to her feet. "We don't have time for this macho posturing. If we're doing this, we do it as a team. No more infighting."

A tense silence filled the room, broken only by the faint hum of the ceiling fan.

Finally, Just'n nodded. "Akemi's right. We've got a mission. Let's focus."

As the team began preparing, Zeke slipped outside for a moment of quiet. The warm Miami air wrapped around him, the sound of distant waves lapping against the shore.

He pulled out his phone and stared at the picture of Autumn he kept as his wallpaper. "Hold on," he whispered. "I'm coming for you."

Inside, Akemi was busy loading her weapons when her phone buzzed. She glanced at the screen, her heart skipping a beat when she saw the name.

Yasmeen: Call me ASAP.

Akemi stepped into the hallway, pressing the phone to her ear. "Yasmeen?"

"There's something you need to know," Yasmeen's voice came through, sharp and urgent. "I've uncovered something … unexpected. About Diego."

Akemi's blood ran cold. "What is it?"

"Not over the phone," Yasmeen said. "Be careful. That's all I'll say for now."

Akemi ended the call, her mind racing. She glanced back toward the living room, where Diego was now laughing with Just'n as if nothing had happened.

Something was wrong, and she was determined to find out what.

The gateway from intelligent energy to intelligent infinity opens
regardless of circumstance on the striking of the hour.
—Law of One

Chapter 34
THE GHOST RETURNS

The sun dipped below the Miami skyline, casting long shadows over the city. The team was gearing up for the Key Biscayne mission, unaware that a ghost from their past had re-entered the game.

Samantha Vargas stepped out of a sleek black Rolls-Royce Ghost parked in a secluded lot overlooking the ocean. Her presence was magnetic, her high cheekbones and flawless porcelain skin radiating a youth that defied her fifty-five years. Her bobbed blond hair framed her striking features, and her dark, almond-shaped eyes carried an unsettling mix of charm and menace.

She wore a tailored white Alexander McQueen blazer with sharp, angular lapels and matching fitted trousers. Her black Christian Louboutin stilettos clicked against the pavement as she walked. Around her neck, a diamond-encrusted Cartier necklace shimmered, catching the fading light. Her lips, painted a deep crimson, curled into a faint smile as she inhaled the salty ocean breeze.

The faint scent of Chanel No. 5 lingered as Samantha approached her sniper team, perched on a nearby rooftop. Dressed in tactical black, they stood at attention, their high-powered rifles pointed at the safe house where Zeke and his team were preparing.

"Report," Samantha said, her voice soft yet commanding, like a blade wrapped in silk.

One of the snipers, a tall man with a scar running down his jawline, handed her a tablet. "They're inside, moving equipment. Diego and Zeke seem to be at odds, but no major action yet."

Samantha's manicured fingers scrolled through the live footage of the safe house. Her sharp eyes narrowed as she spotted Akemi pacing in the background. "Interesting," she murmured.

The sniper hesitated before asking, "Ma'am, do we take the shot if they leave?"

Samantha tilted her head, considering. "Not yet. Let them move. I want to see where they're going. If they lead us to Autumn …" She let the sentence hang, her smile turning into a predatory grin.

Autumn. Her stepdaughter.

Samantha's mind wandered briefly to the fractured relationship she'd shared with Autumn after marrying her father. Their bond was never traditional, and Samantha had often buried any sense of familial loyalty under her cold exterior. Yet, for reasons she didn't fully understand, she felt an obsessive need to keep Autumn under her control. Perhaps it was a remnant of guilt, or perhaps it was something darker.

She turned back to her car, her movements graceful and deliberate. Inside, the air smelled of Italian leather and her signature perfume. Samantha reached for a slim briefcase and pulled out a custom silenced pistol, admiring its weight in her hand.

"I've waited too long for this," she whispered to herself. "I hope Autumn is safe, but no one escapes me."

Her phone buzzed. It was a message from one of her CIA contacts, an old ally from her days in the agency's darker corners. The message was short and cryptic:

They're making moves. Key Biscayne. Your move, Vargas.

Samantha's smile deepened as she tucked the phone back into her blazer pocket. She glanced at her reflection in the car window, adjusting her diamond earrings.

"Let's see how this plays out," she said, stepping back out into the warm Miami night.

Meanwhile, at the Safe House

Zeke felt a chill run down his spine while he loaded his gun. Something about the air felt … off. His heightened senses, his "gift," as Yasmeen liked to call it, he had been on edge all day.

"We need to move," he said to Just'n, who was checking the route to Key Biscayne.

"You think we're being watched?" Just'n asked, raising an eyebrow.

Zeke hesitated, his hazel-green eyes scanning the shadows outside the window. "I don't think. I know."

Inside, Akemi was on her second cup of coffee, her nerves frayed. She glanced at Diego, who was unusually quiet, his phone clutched tightly in his hand.

"Why do you look so guilty?" Akemi asked, her tone sharp.

Diego smirked, but it didn't reach his eyes. "I don't know what you're talking about."

Before Akemi could press him further, Zeke walked in. "We leave in ten minutes. Gear up."

Back to Samantha

As the safe house grew quiet, Samantha stood on the rooftop with her sniper team, watching as Zeke and his crew loaded into their vehicles.

"Follow them," she ordered, her voice cold. "No one engages until I say so."

She turned to the scarred sniper. "And if they find Autumn before I do … ?"

He nodded. "We eliminate them."

Samantha's crimson lips curled into a smile. "Good. Now, let's see if Zeke is as clever as he thinks he is."

As the convoy of vehicles disappeared into the Miami streets, Samantha slipped back into her car. The hunt had officially begun.

Chapter 35

CLOSING THE CIRCLE

The air around the mansion in Key Biscayne carried a charged weight as the sun dipped below the horizon. Zeke's team had secured the perimeter, but the tension was far from over. Inside the crumbling walls, Zeke's heart raced as he followed the faint trail of Autumn's scent, his mind oscillating between hope and fear.

Just'n stayed close to him, his tall frame moving with precision through the dimly lit halls. "You sure she's here, Zeke?" he asked, his voice low but steady.

"She's here," Zeke replied without hesitation. "I can feel it."

In a nearby room, Akemi stood guard, her sharp eyes scanning the darkness. Her grip on her weapon was firm, but her thoughts were elsewhere—on Diego, Yasmeen's departure, and the ever-tightening noose that was Mr. Henderson's influence.

"Zeke's not the only one with unfinished business," she muttered to herself, her voice laced with determination.

Samantha's Final Play

Outside, Samantha's polished heels clicked against the stone path as she approached the mansion's entrance. Her blonde bob framed her face perfectly, her makeup flawless despite the heat. She exuded confidence, her movements calculated and deliberate.

Her phone buzzed again, another update from her sniper team.

They're inside. Zeke's close to finding her.

Samantha smirked, slipping her phone into her jacket. "Good. Let him find her," she said softly. "It's time for the final act."

She motioned for her backup team to stay behind, opting to go in alone. Samantha had a knack for controlling situations, and she wasn't about to lose that now.

The Reunion

Zeke finally found the room at the end of the mansion's east wing. The door was locked, but a swift kick sent it flying open. Inside, Autumn lay strapped to a bed, her body limp but alive. The faint hum of a medical device in the corner revealed she was still being sedated.

"Autumn!" Zeke rushed to her side, his hands trembling as he carefully removed the restraints. Her skin was pale, her breathing shallow, but she was alive.

Just'n entered the room behind him, covering the door. "We need to move—now. This place is compromised."

Zeke nodded, lifting Autumn into his arms. Her head rested against his chest, and for a brief moment, everything else faded away.

"Stay with me," he whispered to her. "I've got you."

The Showdown

As they made their way back to the main hall, Samantha stepped into view, her gun drawn but lowered.

"Well, isn't this a touching reunion," she said, her voice dripping with sarcasm.

Zeke froze, his hazel-green eyes locking with Samantha's icy stare. "Samantha," he said, his voice cold. "What are you doing here?"

"Saving my stepdaughter, of course," she replied with a smirk. "Though it looks like you beat me to it."

Just'n raised his weapon, but Zeke motioned for him to lower it.

"You've been watching us this whole time," Zeke said, his voice laced with accusation. "Why not help sooner?"

Samantha's smile faltered for a moment, but she quickly recovered. "Because I needed to know if you were still the man I trained, Zeke. And it looks like you haven't disappointed."

Her words hung in the air like a challenge, but Zeke didn't have time for games.

"Move," he said firmly.

Samantha stepped aside, her expression unreadable. "We'll meet again," she said as they passed her. "Count on it."

The Escape

Outside, the team regrouped, loading into their SUVs as the mansion erupted into chaos. Henderson's men had arrived, but they were too late to stop the team's escape.

As they sped away, Zeke held Autumn close, his mind racing with plans for their next move.

"We're not safe yet," Just'n reminded him, glancing out the window.

"We will be," Zeke replied, his voice steady. "But first, we're taking her home."

The Pieces Left Behind

Back in Miami, the team regrouped in a secluded safe house. Autumn was recovering slowly, her mind still foggy from the sedatives. Zeke stayed by her side, his resolve stronger than ever.

Meanwhile, Samantha watched from afar, her next move already in motion. She wasn't done with Zeke, not by a long shot.

And in Russia, Yasmeen stood on a snowy balcony, her mind consumed with thoughts of revenge. The hunt for Miami was far from over, and Yasmeen was determined to see it through.

The game wasn't over. It was only just beginning.

Chapter 36

SHADOWS OF INTENT

The Miami skyline glittered against the inky night, alive with the rhythm of its unrelenting pulse. Zeke leaned against the railing of the safe house's balcony, the salty ocean breeze brushing over his face. Inside, Autumn was finally resting, her breathing even and steady. But Zeke's mind was far from calm.

Just'n joined him, his tall frame silhouetted by the dim glow of the city. He handed Zeke a glass of whiskey. "You know this isn't over, right?"

Zeke took the glass, his hazel-green eyes narrowing. "It's never over, Just'n. Not until Henderson and everyone tied to him is gone."

Just'n smirked, but there was no humor in his expression. "You keep saying that, but you're running yourself ragged. You can't save everyone."

Zeke sipped the whiskey, letting the burn remind him he was still alive. "I don't need to save everyone. Just the people that matter."

Yasmeen's Parallel Hunt

Across the globe, Yasmeen was orchestrating her own mission from a lavish penthouse in Moscow. The room was adorned with rich mahogany and gold accents, a stark contrast to the cold and clinical nature of her plans.

She stood by the window, her radiant black hair cascading over her shoulders, as she reviewed the intel her team had gathered. A map of Miami was spread across the glass table before her, with red circles marking key locations.

"Miami," she whispered, her green eyes gleaming. "You can run, but I'll find you."

Her second-in-command, Dimitri, entered the room, holding a folder. "We've tracked her to a shipping hub near the port. It's heavily guarded, but we have a way in."

Yasmeen glanced at the folder, her lips curving into a cold smile. "Perfect. Prepare the team. We move at dawn."

Samantha's Next Move

Back in Miami, Samantha sat in the dimly lit corner of a private club, her designer heels resting on the edge of the table. Her blond bob framed her sharp features as she scanned the room. She was meeting someone tonight—an ally, or at least a resource.

A tall man in a tailored suit approached, his face shadowed by the low light. He slid into the booth across from her, his presence commanding but not threatening.

"You called," he said, his voice deep and smooth.

Samantha leaned forward, her crimson lips curling into a smile. "I need leverage. And you're going to help me get it."

He raised an eyebrow. "And what do I get in return?"

She tapped the folder on the table. "A chance to take down Henderson. For good."

The Team Prepares

Meanwhile, back at the safe house, the group gathered around the dining table, which was now covered in maps, blueprints, and photos. The tension was palpable as Zeke laid out their next move.

"Diego's playing both sides," Zeke said, his voice low but firm. "He thinks he's got the upper hand, but we're going to use him to get closer to Henderson."

Akemi crossed her arms, her expression skeptical. "And how do you plan to do that without him catching on?"

Zeke smirked. "He's predictable. He'll slip up."

Just'n chimed in, his tone cautious. "What about Autumn? She's still recovering. We can't risk her getting caught in the crossfire again."

"She's staying here," Zeke replied. "Dream and Brandon will keep an eye on her."

Akemi scoffed. "And you trust them?"

Zeke shot her a sharp look. "I trust them to protect her. That's all that matters."

The room fell silent, the weight of their mission settling over them.

Later that night, as Zeke stood watch outside the safe house, his phone buzzed with an unknown number. He hesitated before answering.

"Zeke," a familiar voice purred on the other end.

His grip on the phone tightened. "Samantha."

"Miss me?" she teased, her tone dripping with mockery. "What do you want?"

"To talk," she replied. "Face to face. Tomorrow night. I'll send you the details."

Before he could respond, the line went dead.

Zeke stared at the phone, his jaw clenched. Whatever Samantha was planning, it wasn't good.

As dawn broke over Miami, the team geared up for their next mission. The tension was thick, but so was their resolve.

Yasmeen was on the other side of the world, closing in on her target. Samantha was moving her pieces into place, her true motives still shrouded in mystery.

And Zeke? He was ready for war.

Chapter 37

WHISPERS AND REVELATIONS

Zeke's Silent Vigil

The room was still, bathed in the soft glow of the rising sun. Zeke stood in the doorway of Autumn's room, his tall frame tense as his hazel-green eyes softened, gazing at her. Autumn was finally asleep, her body still marked by faint bruises and scars—a testament to what she'd endured. The gentle rise and fall of her chest was the only sign of peace he could cling to.

His mind was racing. The weight of his failures bore down on him, but in this moment, all he could focus on was her.

The sunlight filtered through the window, highlighting Autumn's caramel-toned skin. Her dark hair fanned across the pillow, and for a fleeting second, Zeke imagined a life where none of this chaos existed—just the two of them, somewhere far away.

He clenched his fists at the thought. She deserved more than this. More than him.

The sound of a distant seagull broke his reverie, and he exhaled sharply, running a hand through his bronze locs while the sun glistened on his Brazilian skin. The serenity of the scene fractured while his mind returned to the harsh reality ahead … His sharp jaw tightened as the memory of Diego at the warehouse flashed through his mind. That scent—Autumn's scent—lingering on Diego like a cruel taunt.

"I'll fix this," he whispered, his voice barely audible. "I swear I'll get you out of this."

A faint stir came from the bed, and Zeke stepped back, unwilling to wake her. He needed to prepare for what came next, but for now, he allowed himself this stolen moment of silence, his heart heavy with guilt and determination.

Paris: The Lab on the Outskirts

Far from the chaos in Miami, Paris was deep in the belly of her secret high-tech lab on the outskirts of Atlanta. The sprawling facility was hidden beneath a nondescript warehouse, accessible only through biometric scans and coded sequences.

The lab hummed with the sound of machinery, sleek monitors lining the walls. Paris, dressed in a fitted black jumpsuit, moved with purpose. Her blonde hair was in a nice, sophisticated ponytail, her face illuminated by the glow of the holographic interface in front of her.

"Pull up the most recent intel," she commanded, her voice sharp and steady.

A sophisticated AI system responded, projecting a map of known Henderson assets. The map pulsated with red dots, each representing a location of interest.

"Zoom in on Portland," Paris instructed, narrowing her eyes.

While the map shifted, new images appeared—warehouse schematics, recent shipments, and a grainy security photo of what looked like masked men loading crates.

"Goat heads," she muttered, her stomach churning. She leaned in closer, studying the details. The crates were marked with symbols she hadn't seen before—symbols tied to ancient oceanic mythology.

Her fingers danced across the console while she cross-referenced the symbols with her database. A name popped up: *Poseidon's Shadow.*

Paris frowned, the pieces starting to click into place. This wasn't just about Henderson's empire. This was bigger—global, even.

Her train of thought was interrupted by a sharp beep from the console.

Incoming Call: Kamari Diamond

Paris hesitated before answering. "Kamari, what's up?"

Kamari's voice crackled through the line, her tone urgent. "I've got something. Just sent it to your secure server. You're not gonna believe what I found in Miami."

Paris arched an eyebrow. "You're being cryptic. Spill it."

"Not over the phone," Kamari replied. "Let's just say Henderson's been busier than we thought. Meet me in two days."

Paris sighed. "Fine. But don't keep me waiting."

The call ended, and Paris leaned back in her chair, staring at the map. Whatever Henderson was planning, it was clear he wasn't working alone.

She pressed a button on her comm device. "Initiate lockdown on Sector 7. NOW!!!" she said as she logged out.

The screens flickered off, alarms blaring throughout the facility. Red warning lights pulsed against the cold steel walls, casting eerie shadows.

Paris took a deep breath, steadying herself. She had done her part—for now. But something gnawed at her. Was it too late? Has the breach already begun?

Grabbing her sidearm, she turned on her heel and strode toward the control room. If they wanted a fight, they were about to get one. When Paris exited the lab, her mind raced with possibilities. Meanwhile, in Miami, Zeke stood at the crossroads of his own decisions, the weight of Autumn's recovery fueling his drive.

Two worlds, connected by chaos, secrets, and a relentless hunger for the truth, were about to collide.

To Be Continued …

Will Zeke get the revenge he desires, or will he die trying? Only time will tell what fate has in store for him.

Will Yasmeen forgive Miami for standing her up in Russia? Only time will tell the depths of her patience.

Will Akemi ever Forgive Diego, who had betrayed her trust for the last time? Only the sands of time and Akemi's resolve could authentically answer that question.

Will Agent Dixon stay loyal to Paris and help track down Miami, without pursuing Operation Mongoose? Agent Dixon could almost hear the clock ticking, each second a reminder of his precarious position.

What new intel did Diamond find, and who is the mysterious man who handed her the coordinates?

What awaits Paris in Miami, Florida, and is it time for her to fulfill the mission that she's been putting off for so long? Only the murmur of the ocean and the whispering winds seemed to hold the secrets of her journey.

Who is Deverist? And what is she planning in the city of Paris, hidden beneath the façade of elegance and romance?

What rabbit hole did Carter jump down? And will he find the hidden secrets Tokyo left behind?

Each question dangled like a mysterious thread, weaving a tapestry of intrigue yet untold.

When will the ancient ones come and restore order?

Where is Miami really hiding, and what's really up her sleeve? The city bustled obliviously above, yet those tugging beneath its surface demanded answers.

Why is Kena, a.k.a. Kay Slay, still missing? The last thing we heard was that she was in Dubai! But what's the big secret that keeps her from returning? The shadows of an unfinished story seemed to entwine her fate.

Will Autumn and Teresa fully recover to join the fight? The time to wake from dreams has drawn near, for darkness stirs with heavy intent.

What does Dream have planned for Brandon, Diego, and Mr. Henderson? She still has her eyes on Autumn, and not in a good way. Beneath the glimmer of Atlanta's lights, plans are set in motion, carrying the weight of destinies unraveled.

Will Summer O'Riley/Amy Lyons expose the truth that she already knows? Will she finally stand up to her strict parents and fully take back her independence? The echoes of past decisions loomed large, urging Summer to confront the shadows of her lineage.

AFFIRMATIONS

For the Body
My body is strong, capable, and resilient.
I honor and respect my body's needs.
Every cell in my body is alive with energy and health.
I am grateful for the body that carries me through life.
I nourish my body with love, care, and kindness.
My body is a sacred home, and I treat it with compassion.
I move my body in ways that bring me joy and strength.
Healing flows through me with every breath I take.
I release all judgment and embrace my body's unique beauty.
I am in harmony with my body and listen to its wisdom.

For the Soul
My soul is infinite, radiant, and full of light.
I am deeply connected to the universe and my purpose.
I trust the journey of my soul and embrace its lessons.
Love and peace flow freely within me.
I release all that no longer serves my highest good.
My soul is nourished by joy, creativity, and love.
I embrace my uniqueness and shine my light fearlessly.
I welcome divine wisdom and guidance in my life.
My heart is open to giving and receiving love.
I am whole, worthy, and enough just as I am.

Confidence & Strength
I am strong, capable, and resilient.
I am confident in my abilities and decisions.
I am fearless in the face of challenges.
I am powerful beyond measure.

I am worthy of respect and admiration.

Self-Love & Positivity

I am enough just as I am.
I am deserving of love and kindness.
I am grateful for the person I am becoming.
I am radiant, beautiful, and unique.
I am in harmony with myself and my surroundings.

Success & Abundance

I am attracting success and prosperity.
I am open to limitless possibilities.
I am creating a life of joy and fulfillment.
I am aligned with my highest purpose.
I am worthy of achieving my dreams.

Spiritual Alignment

I am in perfect harmony with the universe.
I am aligned with my highest self.
I am open to divine wisdom and guidance.
I am grounded, centered, and connected to my purpose.
I am flowing effortlessly with the energy of life.

Emotional Alignment

I am balanced in mind, body, and spirit.
I am at peace with where I am and where I am going.
I am releasing resistance and embracing flow.
I am allowing my emotions to guide me with clarity and wisdom.
I am trusting the timing of my life.

Life Alignment

I am walking the path that is meant for me.
I am in alignment with my dreams and goals.
I am attracting the right people, opportunities, and experiences.
I am making choices that support my highest good.

I am living in tune with my soul's purpose.

"Take a deep breath and feel the warmth of life flowing through you. You are a masterpiece, crafted by the universe with intention and love. Every breath you take is a reminder that you are alive, strong, and deeply connected to all that is. You are worthy of love, joy, and peace—not because of what you do, but because of who you are."

—Paris D.

ABOUT THE AUTHOR

Paris D is a visionary storyteller with a flair for crafting dynamic characters and intricate plots that keep readers on the edge of their seats. With a deep passion for blending suspense, drama, and action, Paris D's works are as cinematic as they are gripping. When not immersed in the worlds they create, Paris D channels their creativity into exploring new inspirations, always seeking to push boundaries and elevate their craft. Dedicated to captivating readers with every twist and turn, Paris D invites you into their universe—where nothing is ever as it seems.

Hi, I'm Paris D, and I'm so excited to share my stories with you! Writing has always been my way of diving into worlds full of suspense, action, and unforgettable characters. I love creating plots that keep you guessing and moments that make you feel like you're right there with the characters. My goal is to pull you into a story so deeply that you can't put it down.

When I'm not writing, I'm soaking up inspiration wherever I can find it, always thinking about the next twist, turn, or shocking reveal. Thank you for being apart of this journey with me—I can't wait for you to experience the ride!

OSHUN
ORI CORPORATION